SCRAMBLING INTO THE PIRATE SHIP . . .

Blade flourished both his weapons. The pirate leader died with the rapier jutting out the back of his neck while his own cutlass whistled through the air, inches short of Blade. Another pirate lunged forward past the leader. Blade kicked him in the stomach and laid open his throat with a slash of the dagger as he jerked his rapier free to confront a third opponent.

This one bobbed and weaved, making three of Blade's thrusts miss. Then the pirate sprang in and under the rapier, bringing his cutlass down in a whistling slash that missed taking off Blade's arm. But the pirate was off balance for a moment, long enough for Blade to thrust the dagger into his stomach, then snatch the cutlass out of the air as the man's hand unclasped. Almost with the same motion, he slashed down to take off the head of a fourth attacker trying to get around the dying man.

He had killed four men in something under thirty seconds, and now the men in the boat behind him were waking from their amazement and crowding forward. But a moment later they had their own battle to fight. Out of the corner of his eye Blade saw the second pirate boat sweeping in . . .

THE BLADE SERIES:

#1 THE BRONZE AXE
#2 THE JADE WARRIOR
#3 JEWEL OF THARN
#4 SLAVE OF SARMA
#5 LIBERATOR OF JEDD
#6 MONSTER OF THE MAZE
#7 PEARL OF PATMOS
#8 UNDYING WORLD
#9 KINGDOM OF ROYTH
#10 ICE DRAGON
#11 DIMENSION OF DREAMS
#12 KING OF ZUNGA
#13 THE GOLDEN STEED
#14 THE TEMPLES OF AYOCAN
#15 THE TOWERS OF MELNON
#16 THE CRYSTAL SEAS
#17 THE MOUNTAINS OF BREGA
#18 WARLORDS OF GAIKON
#19 LOOTERS OF THARN
#20 GUARDIANS OF THE CORAL THRONE
#21 CHAMPION OF THE GODS
#22 THE FORESTS OF GLEOR
#23 EMPIRE OF BLOOD
#24 THE DRAGONS OF ENGLOR
#25 THE TORIAN PEARLS
#26 CITY OF THE LIVING DEAD

KINGDOM OF ROYTH

The Richard Blade Series

Jeffrey Lord

PINNACLE BOOKS • LOS ANGELES

BLADE: KINGDOM OF ROYTH

An original Pinnacle Books edition, published for the
first time anywhere.

ISBN: 0-523-40439-5

First printing, March 1974
Second printing, December 1975
Third printing, April 1978

Printed in the United States of America

PINNACLE BOOKS, INC.
2029 Century Park East
Los Angeles, California 90067

KINGDOM OF ROYTH

CHAPTER 1

The official Rolls-Royce carrying J toward the Tower of London was not quite like the advertisements—so quiet that all he could hear was the ticking of the electric clock. But it was almost that quiet, and otherwise there were only faint traffic noises outside. It was eleven o'clock on a spring night, and London was either going to sleep or already asleep.

J would normally have been in bed and asleep also. Part of his rise to the position of head of the special intelligence branch MI6 was the result of years of rising early, not only before the dawn but before his rivals (and his enemies). But tonight Richard Blade was being hurled through Lord Leighton's gigantic computer on his ninth journey into Dimension X. J would sooner have violated the Official Secrets Act than not be on hand when his best agent—almost like a son to him—was hurled off into some fantastic other world to live or die by his own quick wits and superb physical prowess.

Blade had made the same journey eight times. The first time it had been by accident, when an experiment indirectly linking one of Lord Leighton's earlier computers to Blade's mind has gone spectacularly awry. The remaining times, however, his journeys had been part of a deliberately contrived project to explore what was now called Dimension X, for the benefit of England. Over the short time of its existence, Project Dimension X had grown from a bee in Lord Leighton's white-haired bonnet to a massive undertaking housed in a self-contained complex more than two hundred feet below the Tower. Its financing swallowed money to the tune of better than half a million pounds a year. It drew on the talents of some thirty of England's most brilliant men—scientists, engineers, psychologists—without letting them know what they were serving. Only four people in the whole world—J hoped—knew full details. Blade, Lord Leighton, the Prime Minister, and J himself.

In spite of the Prime Minister's generosity with priorities, financing, and staffing, Project Dimension X still had a weak point. That weak point was Richard Blade himself. J grinned wryly at the notion of Blade, with his mind and body and experience, being a "weak point." Then the grin faded.

It was true. Dimension X could not be explored or exploited without somebody going through the computer. So far, the only person able to go through the computer and return alive and sane was Blade himself. One other man had tried; he had returned permanently insane. A dozen others had been considered; all had been rejected. All fell short of Blade's perfection.

But however perfect Blade might be, there was a limit to what he could take. Sooner or later his brain would suffer major damage from too much stress placed on it too often by the computer. Even worse, somewhere out in Dimension X his mighty strength might not be great enough, his lightning reflexes not fast enough, and he would not come back at all.

It was absolutely necessary to find at least one other man, and preferably several, who could survive a trip into Dimension X, both physically and mentally. They needed to take the strain off Blade for his sake. Even more, if he cracked or vanished before they found somebody else, the whole Dimension X project would come to a standstill, possibly for good. That would benefit nobody and nothing.

All of which explained why J was in the official Rolls-Royce heading into London. An hour ago he had been high over the Atlantic in an airliner. To all eyes he had been a tall, elderly impeccably Establishment businessman or civil servant. He had just completed a mission to Washington, a mission personally ordered by the Prime Minister. He had been discreetly inquiring of the Americans whether they had any good agents that might be available for a joint Anglo-American project. Making the inquiries widely enough to get useful information but not so widely that American curiosity was aroused and *they* started inquiring in their turn had been one of the most delicate jobs of J's whole career. He thought it had gone well. At any rate, he already had seven names and the promise of a thorough search of the staffs of American intelligence agencies for more. Between that and the Prime Minister's equally discreet inquiries in England's armed forces, something should turn up.

Of course, it would be preferable for the Project to remain an all-British affair. If the Americans provided men, they would also be sure to demand a share of any benefits from the Project. But even dividing the benefits with the Americans was preferable to suspending the Project entirely. And it was even more preferable to keeping it going with Blade alone until it destroyed him.

J caught himself. Was he thinking too much of saving Blade and not enough of their common duty to England? If he was, it was time to face the fact that he was getting old and hand over his job to a younger, more dispassionate man. Then he remembered that even if he retired as chief of MI6, he would still be involved with Project Dimension X. The Prime Minister had specifically asked him to stay on even after retirement as the Government's representative with the Project. He had agreed. The Prime Minister had tried to present this as a high honor, and J supposed that in a way it was. But, and here he grinned again, it was also an easy way of saving the Prime Minister from having to deal directly with Lord Leighton very often. Leighton might be England's most brilliant scientist, and he might have forgotten more about computers than any other five men in the world had learned. But that didn't make him any less eccentric, irritable, or maddeningly difficult to work with.

J was still running futures—Blade's, his own, and the Project's—back and forth in his mind when the Rolls drew up at the entrance to the Tower. He climbed out, then smiled broadly as a tall figure with an escort of dour Special Branch men loomed up out of the darkness. It was

9

very decent of Richard to come out to meet him here on the surface, even though they couldn't exchange any serious words until they had left the escort behind.

They did that at the massive, gleaming bronze doors marking the head of the elevator shaft down to the complex far below. The door swished shut behind them and the elevator began its unnerving plunge downwards. J turned to Blade and thrust out his hand.

"How are you, Richard? I'm sorry I couldn't get back until just now. I wouldn't have been able to do even that if the P.M. hadn't sent an official car out to the airport for me."

Blade grinned and took the offered hand in a strong grasp. "It wouldn't have mattered. Lord Leighton said we were going to wait before starting the sequence until you arrived, however long that might be."

"Well, I'll be damned!" J's eyebrows rose. "I'm almost prepared to believe that Lord L is developing some human feelings at last."

"Quite possibly. He—" Blade was interrupted as the elevator sighed to a stop. The doors slid open, revealing the familiar long corridor stretching away under the lights.

As they stepped from the elevator, Lord Leighton popped out of a side door like the White Rabbit. He looked even more like an industrious gnome than usual as he scuttled ahead of them down the corridor on his polio-twisted legs. His hunchbacked body bounced inside the grimy white laboratory smock. As they moved along through the familiar series of electronically guarded doors, he kept up a cheerful stream of comment.

"Very glad you could get back in time, J. Richard knew you'd want to be around for the send-off; talked my arm and half my leg off persuading me to wait. No good reason not to, of course. We can start the main sequence any time we choose. The problem's always going to be making adjustments once the sequence is started. So far we haven't had any malfunctions in the middle. We'll have to make some modifications in the sequencing procedure, though. Put in a provision for "holds" like the Americans use on their space launches. Don't want to put

Richard halfway into Dimension X and leave half of him here, do we?"

J found Leighton's cheerfulness more than a trifle ghoulish and his technical comments about as intelligible as if they had been in Chinese. But it again occurred to him—might Leighton possibly be developing some human sensibilities about the whole Project? Was the cheerful patter an effort to conceal a sudden nervousness of his own, as well as to attack the nervousness he assumed J and Blade were feeling? J certainly didn't mind admitting to having the wind up a bit, as usual. He turned to look at Richard, striding along in massive silence beside him. Blade's lips wore a very faint smile, but it seemed to be pasted on, out of keeping with the rest of his manner, which was preoccupied and a bit tense. Hardly surprising, that. Blade had been a first-class field operative for MI6 for the better part of twenty years and had survived more unexpected dangers than most men would encounter in ten lifetimes. But even the worst field assignment didn't throw an agent literally naked into a situation about which he knew absolutely nothing beforehand. So far, Blade's physical and mental qualities had brought him through safely. But this sort of good luck couldn't last indefinitely.

As if he had been thinking along the same lines, Blade turned to J and said, "How was the American mission, sir? Do I plan to retire on my laurels after this trip?" There was a note of self-mockery in Blade's voice that made J feel a little better. Richard was as ready as ever to take whatever the world—this or any other one—might throw at him.

"Don't start planning your retirement yet," J replied in the same light tone. "It's too soon to see if the Americans can come up with anybody good enough. I have a few names, but that's all for the moment. I haven't yet even worked out a proper cover story for bringing them over here for testing."

Blade nodded. "Lord L *thinks* he may be on to a method for the advanced testing of candidates. Not just physically, but mentally as well."

J nodded grimly. He thought of the ruined shell of a

11

man locked away for the remainder of his life in a North County institution because his mind had not survived the trip into Dimension X, even though his body had returned. Lord Leighton turned around and also nodded.

"If the mental breakdown was the result of some physical effect that the computer has on the subject's brain, we're barking up the wrong tree. And if it turns out that Richard is the only man in the world with a brain immune to that effect—well, we're in a nasty situation. But if it's simply a question of a man's being unable to adapt to such a fantastically different environment, one of the psychiatrists thinks he *may* have developed a new method of testing for stress tolerance. If it—ah, here we are."

As always, the main computer room, filled with the great shadowy bulks with their crackled finish and the swarm of writhing multicolored wires reminded J of an abandoned temple of some fantastic and sinister religion overrun by the jungle. And the squat black chair in its glass cubicle in the middle looked like an altar for sacrifices of a highly unpleasant sort.

Blade, however, seemed entirely relaxed and at home. He turned to J and said, "Well, sir, it looks like that time again. No point in making Lord L wait any longer." They shook hands, and Blade stepped into the dressing room.

Inside, he quickly stripped naked and began smearing on the black paste that protected him from electrical burns as the computer's immense power surged through his body. Now that the time was drawing near, he felt his tension slipping away. It was replaced by anticipation. Apart from what it might bring for England, the whole Project offered him an endless series of challenges and adventures. And it was a love of these that had helped bring him into the intelligence service in the first place.

This time, of course, he was not running away from a broken love affair or running toward some place he hoped might cure an inexplicable and maddening impotence. He had resigned himself to a series of fleeting relationships with women as long as he was working on the Project. As for his virility, neither he nor any of his recent partners could have any reasonable complaints on that score. No, it

12

was just a case of going out once more to do what he did well and, when you got right down to it, enjoyed doing.

He pulled on the loincloth. This was purely a gesture, since it had never yet survived the trip. He stepped out into the chamber and strode over to the chair. He knew the routine by now to the point that he felt like twiddling his thumbs as Lord L adjusted the net of restraining straps, then began attaching the cobra-headed electrodes to every part of Blade's body. This went on until he was festooned with wires—blue, green, yellow, red—leading off in every direction into the guts of the computer, like some mad artist's vision of an octopus.

Then there was a further wait, while Blade's impatience began to build. Of course Leighton had to doublecheck everything. Still, why did he always have to be so bloody slow about it? Blade took several breaths as deep as the straps permitted and tried to relax.

Finally everything was ready. J moved aside and raised a hand in farewell as Lord L stepped slowly up to the main console and poised his hand over the master control switch. He turned and looked inquiringly at Blade. "Ready, my boy?"

"Ready, sir."

"Good luck."

The gnarled hand pressed the master switch. There was a hum of surging power, then the shrill wailing of a hundred thousand flutes filled the chamber and made the air turn a liquid green. Everything around Blade turned green too, except for the figures of J and Lord L. They turned blue, then shrank and became dwarfed and monkeylike, scratched themselves and clambered frantically up the face of the computer. The electrodes writhed and twisted and pulled themselves free from his body, turning to snakes as they did so. The snakes wriggled furiously across the floor and swarmed up the face of the computer after the the fleeing monkey figures.

Just as the snakes reached them, the face of the computer itself cracked open in a hundred places. Blade cringed as the great slabs of facing came pouring down on him and then poured through him, and a tangible black-

13

ness flooded out from the vast hole where the computer had been, gushing out until Blade was completely surrounded by it and the snakes and monkeys were both gone.

Then the blackness receded slightly, and Blade was standing on a concrete block with harsh blue lights pouring down on him from all around. A voice was chanting tonelessly, "Five-four-three-two-one-LIFT-OFF!" Fire spewed out from under the block and he and it together began to rise into the sky. Quickly they were out of the blue lights, rising again into thick blackness, until the flames gushing from the block died and it fell away. Blade hurtled alone through the dark, then felt himself slowing. His climb ceased; he rolled over and began to fall, silently, with no sensation of air rushing past or of anything except the falling, the endless falling.

CHAPTER 2

Blade suddenly realized that he had made the transition into Dimension X. The fall was now a real, physical one. Before he had even had time to wonder where he was going to come down, he hit water with a tremendous splash. He plunged deep enough for the light to turn green, then kicked his way to the surface. The water was cool enough for the coolness to be noticeable, but not enough for it to be uncomfortable. That was fortunate. He might have landed in the local equivalent of the Arctic Ocean, in which case he would have been dead within three minutes. Even so, this was the first time he had found himself in water immediately after a transition.

Treading water, he took stock of the situation as he had done eight times before. As always, he had a splitting headache. And as always, the loincloth had gone, leaving him as naked as any fish that might swim in this—river, lake, sea?—where he had landed. He licked his lips. Salt. So it was an ocean or sea. Next question: how far was he

14

from shore? He was a powerful swimmer—twenty miles was nothing to him—but if he was out in the middle of something the size of, say, the Atlantic Ocean, he was in a sticky situation. Before, it had been a question of landing in the middle of battles or at least of some inhabited territory where he had to fight or at least communicate with the local inhabitants immediately. Now, half his problem was the *lack* of people.

The headache had faded enough now so that he could raise his head and look around. The sea was calm, broken only by a gentle swell no more than two or three feet high. Above its surface nothing moved except the faintest of breezes. The air itself was warm and moist, faintly scented with something Blade at first had trouble identifying. Then he realized it was the smell of smoke. Smoke? In the middle of an ocean? He resumed his scanning of the horizon—not far away, for a man in the water.

It was apparently late afternoon, with a westering sun sliding down from a flawless blue sky. But the western horizon itself had sprouted several tall columns of smoke, coiling greasily straight up into the sky for hundreds of feet before they plumed out at the top into broad, feathery clouds. There was the source of the smoke odor, but what lay at the base of those columns and clouds was invisible just beyond the horizon. Still, whatever might be there was more likely to be a source of help than the empty ocean nearer at hand. Or at least it could provide information about what sort of beings inhabited this particular Dimension. Steadily, taking his time and conserving his energy, he began to swim towards the smoke columns.

It was well over an hour before what lay at the base of the columns lifted over the horizon. Drifting sluggishly on the sea, five ships were burning. Around them like scum on a stagnant pond floated a wide circle of wreckage—spares, rigging, planking, chests and boxes, overturned boats human bodies. Blade was elated. Here *was* a better chance of survival than swimming about aimlessly in the sea. He quickened his strokes. In a few more minutes, he reached the fringes of the circle, climbed on to the bottom

15

of an overturned boat and looked more closely at the burning ships.

He now noticed that they were of two distinctly different kinds. Two of them were large, broad-beamed merchantman types, with high castles fore and aft and bluff bows. As far as he could tell from what he could see through the smoke and what the battle had left standing, they had possessed two masts, with two or possibly three square sails on each.

The other three ships were smaller, low-slung, with jutting bows apparently ending in rams. They also had two masts, but lanteen-rigged, and there were definitely oar ports in their low sides amidships.

Merchantmen and war galleys—two distinct types. Two distinct sides perhaps? And with all five ships on fire, and wreckage and bodies littering the sea, that suggested a recent battle. Blade found himself scanning the horizon again. The survivors of such a battle, if any, might not be welcome company for a man naked and unarmed. It was time to see what he could scrounge in the way of survival gear from the flotsam spread out over more than a square mile of ocean.

The boat was far too heavy in its waterlogged condition for Blade to right it by himself. But there were plenty of floating spars trailing rigging and still half-wrapped in sails. Kicking hard with his feet, he pushed two such together, added a third, then tied them together with as much rope as he could salvage without a knife to cut it. After half an hour's work, he had a ramshackle raft, three feet wide and about fifteen feet long. It rode half-submerged, like a floating log. But it saved him from having to swim or tread water continuously. And in the course of assembling his raft, he found a small piece of timber that balanced well enough in his hand to make a serviceable club.

The sun was noticeably lower in the sky now. One of the galleys finally dipped its bow under and sank with a great hissing as the fires were drowned and a great bubbling and gurgling as the last of the air escaped from the vanishing hull. Bits of charred wood popped to the surface in the disturbed water it left behind. One of the merchantmen was also visibly lower in the water. The sight of the sinking ship and the thought of oncoming night reminded Blade of the need to get himself a better weapon than the improvised club and, if possible, clothing as well. In the darkness, any survivors of the battle returning to the scene would probably be in a "strike first and ask questions afterwards" frame of mind. Blade didn't blame them, but neither did he want to be a helpless victim. He slid off the raft and swam toward the nearest of the floating boxes and chests. He hoped it hadn't belonged to the captain's mistress and so was full of her cheap jewelry and by now thoroughly waterlogged cosmetics.

The first box he opened was far from useless, though not quite as useful as one containing weapons. It held bolts of coarse, garishly colored cloth, like burlap bags dyed purple, bright blue, red-orange. Trade goods for some primitive tribes somewhere on the remote shores of the ocean? Blade could not help speculating about the people of this Dimension, little evidence though he had as yet to go on. He appropriated the blue cloth and with a good deal of effort—it was tougher than he had anticipated—improvised a loincloth and a rough hood for his head and shoulders, which were already beginning to sting from their exposure to the sun.

He was no longer naked, but he was still practically weaponless, and there were other boxes and chests and crates to examine. Some had been opened already; most of these were as empty as a scraped-out bowl. Others had stout bolts or locks, and he could not swing his club hard enough to smash them open while he was in the water. He had to laboriously push them over to the raft, hoist them on to it and precariously balance both them and himself while he hammered away at the fastenings. He usually fell off two or three times while working on each box, and the box itself usually slipped off the raft into the sea at least once. It was well into twilight, with a raw red and orange glow sprawling across the western horizon, and his own temper blazing nearly as brightly as the sunset, before he finally found what he was looking for.

17

The chest had not been completely filled with weapons, or it would probably have sunk with the weight of the metal inside. Apparently it had held the personal possessions of an officer of one of the ships—colored tunics, white breeches, a belt, a pair of black boots, linen underclothing, a green silk sash, a small enameled brass box for valuables, all jumbled together as though somebody had been hastily pawing through the chest before abandoning ship.

But there was also a sword—a rapier, all point, light and supple, and not a ceremonial weapon. The steel of the blade was good and the hilt and guard plain heavy brass without fancy ornamentation. He flexed the blade experimentally and tried a few thrusts. It would serve quite well against any opponent who wasn't wearing enough body armor to stop the point. And Blade had enough confidence in his own skill with weapons to believe he could find chinks in armor into which to drive the point.

Now he had weapons and clothing of sorts, but no food or water. He was prepared to survive several weeks without food, or with only what he could catch from the ocean. But he had to find some water before another two days had gone by. He would not be dead by then, but he would be almost past the point of being able to save himself, and perhaps to the point of making some foolish mistake (like drinking salt water) that would finish him off quickly. Unfortunately, finding water was probably going to be difficult. He would not be likely to see it bobbing about in chests or boxes in the ocean. Possibly some of the water barrels in the holds of the ships were still intact.

He turned back to the ships, which he had largely ignored during his hunt for survival gear. Another of the galleys had gone down, and one of the merchantmen was so low in the water that Blade knew she also had only a few more minutes afloat. The other merchantman was still blazing too brightly to make it safe to board her. But the remaining galley had burned herself out and was floating, a charred and smoldering hulk, but yet one which might be boarded and even explored safely.

It was now almost dark, with only a faint pearly sheen

in the western sky to mark the final fading of daylight. Blade recalled that in the tropical seas of Home Dimension, nightfall meant large, hungry fish roaming about, seeking what or whom they might devour. This felt like a tropical ocean; he hoped the parallel would not extend farther. It case it did, however, it was time he got moving.

The burning merchantman was spreading a pool of golden light across the surface of the sea, and as Blade turned, his superb peripheral vision caught something moving on the outer fringes of that pool. He froze, turning only his head to get a better look. Then he slowly flattened himself on his raft.

A boat was rowing out of the darkness toward the floating hulks and wreckage—a ship's boat, crowded with men and rowing about five oars a side. They were rowing very badly, Blade noticed, with much splashing and catching of crabs. The oarsmen were either untrained or nervous or both. However, that wasn't an important question. They were other human beings. Unfortunately, there was no way of knowing which side they belonged to. At least neither side had any compelling reason to be violently hostile to him, the proverbial innocent bystander. And these people were certainly a better alternative than either exploring smoldering hulks in search of water or sitting on his raft until he died of thirst. He took a firm grip on the rapier, stood up and HALOOOOED at the top of his powerful lungs.

The sound carried well over the water to the boat. Blade saw it suddenly swing around as the oars stopped. There was a dead silence that lasted until Blade wondered if his hail had stricken everyone in the boat mute or dead. Then a harsh shout came back over the water.

"Who goes there?"

Blade was no longer surprised at his ability to understand and speak the local language from his first moment in a new Dimension. Lord Leighton of course found it a fascinating psychological and physiological phenomenon and had once devoted several hours to an enthusiastic and, to Blade, totally unintelligible consideration of the various possible explanations for it. He shouted back.

19

"Friend!"

There were audible mutterings in reply to this, followed by another moment's silence. Then someone shouted an order and the boat swung back on course towards Blade, the oars splashing away as busily and as sloppily as before. In five minutes the boat was close enough for Blade to make out its occupants clearly—and for them to make him out also. At that point the boat stopped again. Blade grinned as he realized that this must be the result of his own appearance. If these were the survivors of the battle, the sight of a huge man whose near nakedness revealed massive muscles and whose hand held a long and businesslike rapier would understandably be enough to make them hold back. He lowered the rapier to the raft and spread both hands out in a conciliatory gesture.

"I said 'Friend,' damn you! What do I look like?"

That started the mutterings off again. He even heard one or two laughs. Apparently they couldn't make up their minds. Finally, one man, bare to the waist but with the air of a leader about him, stood up and shouted across.

"What was your ship, fellow?"

"None of these." Blade gestured at the hulks. "I hail from the south. My ship sank two days ago."

"Howfor it sank? No storms this part of t'ocean of late. Or did ye meet pirates too?"

"Pirates?"

"By Druk's sea-green beard, you're from a distant land if ye've no heard o' the pirates of Neral." The man's eyes narrowed. "Less'n ye be one yourself. Forbye—" and he began to rattle off a stream of words that Blade guessed must be some sort of slang. He went on until the blank incomprehension—partly natural, partly assumed—on Blade's face brought him to a stop. Then he shrugged. "If ye be not knowing the Neralers' cant, ye be none of them, tho' who ye be else I know not. Throw me over that pigsticker ye be wavin', and then swim over to us bare as a babe. I'll be leavin' no seaman here for the Neralers if they come back. But I'll not be riskin' my men either."

Blade complied. When he was safely in the boat, the

20

man looked him over again carefully and said, "Ye look like no man I've ever seen, but Druk's not a liker of sailors who abandon a man to the sea or the Neralers. Still, ye'll be sittin' quiet and makin' no moves for a weapon, or ye'll be spitted and fed to the fishes. If—"

"Brora! Look!" somebody behind them shouted. Blade and the other man spun about to see two low-slung boats swing out from behind the abandoned galley and move towards them. Blade knew instinctively that these were the Neral pirates Brora had mentioned. He also realized that if they found him in a boatload of their enemies, they would kill him along with the rest before he could explain who he was. Even a chance to explain might not do him any good. It was time to fight.

Brora was shouting to his men. There were clatters and scrapings of metal as swords and daggers were drawn. He raised his hands to heaven and bellowed, "Druk, save us now!" and muttered under his breath, "Why did we come back like a pack o' fools?" Blade took advantage of the distraction to snatch up his rapier. Brora turned, started, glared at Blade.

"Damn it, Brora, I *told* you I was a friend! The pirates will kill me just as readily as they will you! Don't waste your time distrusting me!" Brora frowned, but then nodded and handed Blade a dagger. The pirates were almost up to them now. There was no room to run, only to fight.

If the pirates had had arrows, the fight would have been hopeless. But they had only the same swords and knives as their opponents, so they had to close. As the two pirate boats moved in, oars thumping in a trained rhythm, Blade rose from the bottom of the boat to a half crouch and stared at them, trying to guess their tactics.

One boat was going to cut off their retreat; it was swinging around behind them. The other was coming straight in at full speed. In a moment Blade knew it was going to plough into them, trying to capsize them. But Brora knew his business. He yelled to the oarsmen, and they snatched up the oars. Clumsy though they were, their frantic efforts pivoted the boat around.

The boats met bow to bow with a crash and a shock that threw practically everybody in both off their feet with curses and a clatter of weapons. Practically everybody— except Blade. Before the pirate crew could regain their feet, he was over the side of their boat, flourishing both his weapons.

The pirate leader had been ready to lead his men into the enemy's boat, so he was the first to die. Blade's longer weapon and immensely longer reach gave him a decisive advantage. The pirate leader died with the rapier jutting out the back of his neck while his own cutlass whistled through the air futile inches short of Blade. Another pirate lunged forward past the leader. Blade kicked him in the stomach and laid open his throat with a slash of the dagger while jerking his rapier free to confront a third opponent.

This one bobbed and weaved, making three of Blade's thrusts miss by inches. Then the pirate sprang in and under the rapier, bringing his cutlass down in a whistling slash that missed taking off Blade's arm but crashed into the guard of the rapier so hard that it flew out of Blade's hand and over the side. But the pirate was off balance for a moment, long enough for Blade to thrust the dagger into his stomach, then snatch the cutlass out of the air as the man's hand unclasped. Almost with the same motion he slashed down to take off the head of a fourth pirate trying to get around the dying man.

He had killed four men in something under thirty seconds, and now the men in the boat behind him were waking from their amazement and crowding forward. But a moment later they had their own battle to fight. Out of the corner of his eye Blade saw the second pirate boat sweeping in. With a crash it smashed into the merchant sailors' boat, pushing it away from the first pirate boat. With yells and howls its crew hurled themselves on their opponents.

Blade was too busy to watch any more of that. He was alone in the bow of the first boat now, alone against eight or ten armed and furious pirates. The cutlass was shorter and heavier than the rapier, but it had an edge as well as a point. He chopped down with it like a butcher chopping

22

meat while the dagger flickered in and out. The pirates could only get at him one or two at a time without going over the side. One bolder or more imaginative type tried that. But as the man rolled himself over the side of the boat into the water, Blade parried a thrust with his dagger, slashed his current opponent across the belly with a cutlass stroke, and leaped across the falling body to bring the cutlass up, over, and down on the bold one's back. He felt the blade chop through the spine. The man went limp and rolled into the water with a splash, vanishing like a lead statue.

There were eleven bodies in the boat when Blade finished, and the bottom was awash two inches deep in blood. If there had been any survivors of the crew, they had thrown themselves over the side and thrashed frantically off into the darkness to get away from this monster that had hurled himself upon them. Gradually, as the fury of battle faded from his mind, Blade became aware of someone calling.

"Hoy, friend! Be ye hurt? By Druk's coral trident, that were fightin' like none ever seen!" Blade turned about and saw Brora standing in his own boat some twenty yards away, surrounded by the survivors of his own men. Another thirty yards beyond, the second pirate boat was limping off, only two or three raggedly plied oars on each side in action, and blood visible on some of the oarsmen. Brora saw Blade looking, and grinned savagely. "Aye, they be goin'. We were hard at it for a bit, but we took six or seven o' them to four of us. Then they saw what ye'd done o'er there and that were enough for 'em. Hold where ye be, friend. We'll come clean those sharks out o' their boat and take it for our own."

After the dead pirates had been stripped of usable gear and clothing and dumped over the side, the merchant sailors redistributed themselves among the two boats. While this was going on, Brora drew Blade as much out of earshot as possible and looked hard at him, with a faint smile on his weatherbeaten face.

"From the south, ye say?"

23

Blade shrugged. "As much as any place. "I'm a foot-loose type by nature."

"And a fighter. I've seen no sailor who could fight like that, tho' we do reckon ourselves fair tough in any scrap."

"I wasn't a sailor. Down south—" Blade hoped there was enough of a "south" in this Dimension to make his story plausible "—I *was* a professional soldier. A free-lance. There are many such."

"So I hear," said Brora, and that was apparently as much as he was interested in inquiring into Blade's origins. "Well, I tell ye—whatever ye think ye be worth as a fighter, any shipmaster of Royth would give ye double it or more were ye to sign on w' him as a guard. Ye've seen what the pirates are like. 'Tis a miracle sent by Druk to aid honest sailors that we found ye." He thrust out his hand. "Brora Lanthal's son swears friendship with ye from now 'til death divides us. What say ye?"

Blade clasped the hand and shook it vigorously. "I say yes, Brora."

"Well and good. When Brora speaks, no few o' the Sailor's Guild listen. And we sailors be half the honest men of Royth these days." Before Blade could ask any further questions, Brora turned away and began issuing orders about shifting supplies and raising sail. Blade took the chance, a welcome one, to sit down and rest.

CHAPTER 3

Blade had plenty of time to rest and think in the five days before they were picked up. Unfortunately, little of the thinking led to any useful conclusions. During the whole five days all he could guess from the conversation and from what Brora told him was that the Ocean was surrounded by land. Most of the land was divided among four kingdoms. Of these kingdoms, the most powerful was the Kingdom of Royth, from which Brora and his men came. In the Ocean, however, also stood the island of

Neral, somewhat to the north of their present position. It was the base for a powerful confederacy of pirates, almost a fifth kingdom in military power, which preyed on the shipping and even on the coasts of the Four Kingdoms. During the past five years, the pirates had been growing more numerous, more enterprising, and more ferocious.

Brora had been first mate aboard the *Blackfish*, the larger of the two merchantmen Blade had seen burning. Because both ships were larger than usual, and both had well-armed and determined crews, they had succeeded in sinking one of the pirate galleys outright and setting the other three hopelessly on fire before themselves going up in flames. This, Brora emphasized, was a very unusual outcome for a battle against the pirates of Neral. They usually won, taking the ship and cargo, and either murdering, enslaving, recruiting, or (very rarely) holding for ransom everybody aboard. The survivors of both sides had made off in their boats, too concerned at first with sheer survival to bother each other. But Brora had decided that it might be wise to return to the area of the battle, to pick up any salvageable gear that might prove useful for survival. Apparently the remaining pirates had had the same idea. Thus the encounter.

A passing rain squall had given them several more days' worth of water and one of the sailors had set several lines over the side for fish. Brora estimated that with reasonable luck with the weather they would reach shore within three weeks. They were unfortunately farther south than merchant ships on the east-west route usually sailed, so it was not too likely that they would be picked up. But they were in no immediate danger, except for the possibility of more pirates or storms. Blade went to sleep that night in a resigned but relaxed frame of mind.

So it was an agreeable surprise when he was awakened the next morning by cries from the sailors.

"A ship! A ship!"

As always, Blade was fully awake in an instant. He sat up, turned, and looked at the approaching ship. It was already hull-up, and even at a distance he could see that it was enormous, with three tall masts each carrying three

25

square sails and a fourth mast with a single triangular lateen sail perched aft. The high-sided hull gleamed with gilding and dark blue and red paint.

"That's a ship of Royth, sure enough," muttered Brora. "A royal warship, indeed." He looked vaguely disturbed as he said that.

"Is that unusual?" asked Blade.

"Nay, nay. Royth has a good fleet, tho' no as large as it ought to be, for the safety o' her coasts and shipping. But ye seldom see a royal warship sailin' by herself in these waters. Ay well, there's naught to be gained by frettin' over what we can't help." He turned away to rummage a signal rocket out of its tarred-canvas casing in the bottom of the boat, leaving Blade to wonder again what those cryptic remarks might mean. Brora, he had already discovered, was a man who was very sparing with words.

If Brora had intended to imply that the ship might be a pirate's prize, he was wrong. The signal rocket arched up and went off in a flurry of green smoke. A few minutes later another rocket rose up in reply from the ship as she came about. Half an hour later they were alongside her. Blade stared up at the immense height of her sides to the peak of her tallest mast, where a black banner with five red castles in a circle on it flapped limply in the light breeze. Bearded faces lined the rails, most of them topped with leather or metal helmets, and Blade saw the glint of spear points and sword blades.

Somebody stuck a black-bearded face farther over the railing and yelled down:

"Ahoy, the boat! Who be ye?"

"Survivors of Krim's *Blacksnake*. She and Malfor's *Trident* met pirates not far from here six days a-gone. Both burned, but we sank one pirate and burned t'other three."

Cheers exploded from the deck above at Brora's words. Beardface was silent, though, and shouted back:

"Can ye prove this? We know not if'n ye be pirates yourselves, set adrift to be picked up and betray us from wi'in." The cheers died, to be replaced by apprehensive grumbling.

26

"WHAAAAT?" exploded Brora. "By Druck's sea-weed-covered prick, I'll skin ye for that! Know ye not Brora Lanthal's son?"

More muttering and grumbling. Then the crowd of faces at the railing gave way as a tall gray-haired man stepped into view and stared down at the boat with piercing black eyes. He wore a black tunic with the same five red castles on the chest as Blade had seen on the ship's banner. Blade had the sensation of being under an abnormally keen and intelligent scrutiny.

Brora took one look at the man and quickly knelt. "My Lord Duke! This then be your ship?"

"Yes, but why I am aboard it and it is here is a story best told before fewer ears." The duke glared about him and Blade saw most of the heads abruptly disappear. "Captain, I know this Brora Lanthal's son. He and any with him have my countenance as honest men."

"But m'lord—" began the bearded face who had first spoken.

"Captain, I am still a Grand Duke of Royth," said the duke coldly. Blade saw the captain's mouth shut abruptly. Moments later a rope ladder sailed over the railing and dropped down the side of the ship. And a few moments after that, Blade, Brora, and the other ten men from the boat were standing securely on the ship's deck, just forward of the mainmast.

CHAPTER 4

The man in black turned out to be the Grand Duke Khystros, younger brother to King Pelthros of Royth. Blade was sufficiently self-assured to feel no uneasiness at confronting such a high-ranking individual in his burlap loincloth and sunburned skin. And Khystros had a relaxed, no-nonsense manner that set everybody else at ease, from Brora on down to the youngest ship's boy among the survivors.

After a few sharp questions, Khystros ordered the first mate to take the other survivors forward and see that they were fed, clothed and attended. Then he led Blade, Brora, and the captain down into his own cabin aft. There he dismissed the waiting attendants. With his own hands he rummaged clothing, shoes, and salves out of huge brass-bound chests racked along one wall of the cabin. After that, he sat down in a light folding chair of delicately carved wood and black canvas, fixed Brora with an inquiring glance, and said:

"Well, Brora Lanthal's son. I judge you have a tale to tell. I'm listening."

Brora had been as nervous as a patient in a dentist's waiting room at the prospect of being questioned by such an exalted person. But under Khystros' calming influence, he told his story completely, quickly, and well. The duke mostly listened in silence, only injecting a question now and then. When Brora had finished, the duke nodded his thanks and turned to look at Blade.

"Well, Master—Blahyd?" He pronounced it in two syllables, and Blade realized that he would have to go through this Dimension answering to this mispronunciation.

"That's close enough, sir."

"No doubt. You claim to be a footloose mercenary from the south—a rather vague place of origin, I must say. Are there many like you—in the 'south'?" The duke's skepticism about Blade's story was evident in his voice.

Blade knew he had only a split second to decide how to answer. Khystros' keen wits would detect the slightest hesitation on his part, and then the fat would be in the fire. He put the thought aside, took a deep breath, and said, "Not many, sir. I'm better than most."

"One rather hopes so," said the duke drily. "If the south—or wherever you hail from—is swarming with fighting men who can kill a dozen Neral pirates singlehandedly, a southern army could gobble up all the Four Kingdoms *and* the island of Neral as easily as a cat gobbles up a mouse. However, that's not our concern now." He turned his head slightly. "Alixa! Some wine for our guests, if you please."

The woman who came out of the curtained doorway at the rear of the cabin was obviously Khystros' daughter. The family resemblance was unmistakable. She was as tall as her father, only a few inches shorter than Blade, who was well over six feet, and as slim and fine-boned as a thoroughbred horse. The face framed by great masses of blue-black hair was high-cheeked, with a broad mobile mouth now curved in a welcoming smile and large gray eyes that were appraising Blade with frank interest. She was silent as she sped about the cabin, taking down leather wine bottles and chased silver cups, filling the cups, and handing them to the three men. Then she folded herself gracefully down onto a cushion by the door and listened while her father explained to Blade the sad situation of the Kingdom of Royth and of himself as well.

The pirates of Neral were indeed waxing stronger and fiercer each month and year, as Brora had said. Never before, in fact, had so large a force as the four galleys that had attacked *Blacksnake* and *Trident* been seen so far south. It was good that the pirates had paid so heavily for their victory. Perhaps this would make them think before sending a squadron so far afield again.

But it would take far more than one affair of mutual slaughter to beat back the threat from Neral forever. The pirate island was the base for some two hundred warships plus supporting vessels, manned by some fifty thousand or more fighting men and women. But there was more than the sheer military might of the pirates involved in their threat. In fact, that might was seriously flawed by the pirates' lack of training and experience in land warfare.

But what if their road were smoothed for them by treachery? That was another story. And there was treachery afoot in Royth itself. Khystros had no proof of this certain enough to lay before King Pelthros. But he knew to his own complete satisfaction that Count Indhios, High Chancellor of the Kingdom of Royth, was in the pay of the Neralers. It was obvious that if the pirates could take, by force or treachery, one of the Four Kingdoms and add

29

its resources to their own, they would become the rulers of the Ocean and arbiters of the fate of all who lived by it or traveled on it. The stakes in the game they were playing were enormous, but so was the prize they might win.

But Pelthros was not a strong or decisive ruler. He was exceedingly well-intentioned and concerned about justice, to be sure, but he failed to realize that justice is not always best rendered by putting off decisions. He also had definite abilities as a craftsman—jewelry-making in particular, which he pursued as often as possible, and too often for the good of his realm.

All this (which Khystros mentioned with an apologetic air, knowing it ill became him to criticize his monarch and brother in such a fashion) had much bearing on Khystros' situation. When the duke had first broached the notion of the Chancellor's treachery to Pelthros, he had been told sharply to go back and gather more evidence before he would be allowed to confront a high and long-trusted servant of the crown with such a monstrous charge. That had given Indhios the time he needed.

The Chancellor in his turn had brought forward cleverly manufactured evidence that Khystros was conspiring to make off with a large portion of the royal taxes by appointing his own subjects as tax collectors. And what was he planning to do with the money? Ah, that was as yet something of a mystery. But certainly Khystros would only need such vast sums of money beyond his already great wealth if he needed to pay a faction among the nobility. For what end, who knew?

Pelthros was naturally even less willing to arraign his own brother on inadequate evidence than he was his Chancellor. But Indhios had suggested an alternative course of action. Khystros had been reproaching himself ever since for not having suggested it first; he felt his failure showed great want of statecraft.

On the eastern shore of the Ocean lay the Kingdom of Mardha, the largest though poorest of the Four Kingdoms. What better way to improve relations between Mardha and Royth than by sending King Pelthros' own honorable brother there as Ambassador, with his daughter and a suitably chosen retinue? In far-distant Mardha, Khystros could perform a valuable service to his Crown, yet have little time and less opportunity for plotting and faction-building.

"So here I am," finished Khystros. "I could hardly refuse, because that would have played into Indhios' fat hands. I did suggest that to be less conspicuous I travel in a small, fast vessel, with only my daughter and a few guards and secretaries. But Indhios convinced my brother that the High King of Mardha sets great store by an imposing show. Were I to appear in anything less than the chief warship of the royal fleet of Royth, with less than a hundred useless mouths in my train, both I and the Kingdom would be forever disgraced in the eyes of the Mardhans. Ah, well, we must eat what is set before us."

He looked sharply at Blade again. "Wherever you come from, it seems clear to me that you have no love for the pirates. You are a fighting man such as one meets more often in legend than in fact. And Mardha is a wild land, with its High Kings barely able to keep order even within the walls of their own palaces. What do you say to joining my service as a guard? You deserve more rank than I could give you without arousing jealousy among those who already serve me, for I can see you are born to lead as well as to fight. But in Mardha, anything may happen, and the more trustworthy men I have guarding my back, the better I will feel. Well, Master Blahyd?"

Blade had to consider the offer only for a moment. He could hardly find a position that offered better opportunities to explore this world than that of a household guard to an important and far-traveling noble. Furthermore, he could make use of his great skill in combat and would have no need to support himself by pretending to other skills he did not possess. And of all the masters he had found it necessary or expedient to serve in his travels, Khystros seemed among the most decent. So he nodded and then added, "What about Brora Lanthal's son? We are sworn friends."

Khystros grinned. "I was about to offer him a place also. Seamaster Brora, you served well aboard the yacht

31

of my wife's father in your younger days. Will you serve me as well now?"

"I will, sir."

"So be it." Khystros refilled the wine cups, and they all drank.

CHAPTER 5

For over a week the ship, *Triumph*, sailed east before the light but steady breeze. Brora and the other survivors of the battle were quickly accepted into the crew and assigned duties. Brora became an assistant to the sailing master; others took posts as their skills suggested. Blade, as one of the Grand Duke's private guard, had no shipboard duties, but exercised regularly in arms with the other guardsmen. They were indeed few. Most of the Grand Duke's retainers were useless civilian hangers-on, seasick half the time even in the good weather and seldom appearing on deck. Blade shuddered to contemplate what would happen to those poor wretches in the event of a pirate attack.

Blade's superb physique quickly threw off the minor effects of his five days adrift. The other guards were frankly amazed at what he could do with rapier and dagger, broadsword, battleaxe, or mace. None of them could best him, and few could even stay with him in the canvas-covered arms arena marked out amidships for more than a few minutes at a time. Practice sessions, simple but ample meals, and sleep to throw off the healthy exhaustion of much hard physical exercise took up much of the day. But there was still time for Blade to walk the white-scraped planks of *Triumph's* deck, from forward to aft and back again, look up at the sails and masts towering against the searing blue sky, and contemplate his problems.

Apart from simple boredom, there were two of them. There was *Triumph's* captain, and there was the Lady Alixa. Blake had watched the captain's face during the discussion of the pirate danger. The man was clearly skilled at concealing his emotions. But there had been many occasions during Blade's years as a secret agent when reading another man's expression had been a matter of life or death. Blade had trained himself to penetrate disguises and would have sworn the captain was delighted at the news of pirates roaming and ravaging far south of their usual haunts. Furthermore, it seemed entirely plausible to Blade that Chancellor Indhios had bribed or coerced the captain into making sure that Grand Duke Khystros never reached Mardha alive. Whether the captain himself was also in the pay of the pirates and sworn to lead this rich prize like a lamb into the jaws of the wolves was another nasty question.

Unfortunately, there was nothing he could do about his suspicions. He was in the same position as the Grand Duke himself had been in accusing the Chancellor——he had no evidence that would convince a reasonable man. And in a way he was worse off than the duke, since he had no position here that would at least assure him an open, let alone a receptive, ear. He was, he had to face it, nothing but a hired bodyguard. The duke's favor to him might easily dry up if he started hurling what might well seem wild accusations.

The problem with Lady Alixa seemed almost equally insoluble. In a word, she had her eyes on him. He guessed that she was a strong-willed, hot-tempered young woman who would not take kindly to a refusal. She would find some way to make even as levelheaded and just a man as her father believe that Blade had seduced or at least insulted her. And there would go his position, if not his head. Yet if he took her, and Khystros found out, wouldn't the same thing happen? Blade had a reasonably good opinion of himself in general, but he honestly could not see himself as Khystros' choice of a son-in-law. And this was entirely apart from the fearful complications that such a relationship would involve when it came time for him to return to Home Dimension. He had left lovely women and even children behind him on several of his journeys and did not wish to do so again.

33

So he paced the deck and turned steadily browner under the tropical sun that beat down day after day. He learned to identify the seabirds and the great silver and green fish that often paced the ship for hours on end, further toughened his iron physique with more weapons exercise and gymnastics, and occasionally spoke with Khystros. The man seemed to be brooding about something. Blade only hoped it wasn't his daughter's regard for the new guardsman that was troubling the Grand Duke. The Lady Alixa took little care to conceal the look in her eyes when they fell on Blade.

An evening came, when the sun set in a western sky as flawless as ever. But the wind was brisker; flurries of white crowned the rising waves, and the groan and creak of massive timbers and the whine of the wind in the rigging came louder than usual to Blade's ears as he walked aft. Tonight was his turn to guard the door of the Grand Duke's suite, a duty rotated among the guardsmen. He wore a boiled leather cuirass and helmet heavy enough to stop most blades but not subject to rusting in the damp sea air. He carried a straight broadsword and a heavy dagger. A long red cloak with a black lining flowed from his broad shoulders to the tops of his sea boots.

The moon rose, sickle-thin and pale, but the wind held steady. The last light drained from the western sky and the masts and sails faded to vague blurs in the darkness. Blade shifted his weight from one foot to the other for the twentieth time and pulled gently on the well-oiled sword to make sure it rested easily in its scabbard.

Then a soft voice called out behind him.

"Master Blahyd!"

He knew what he would see when he turned around, but still there was a shock in seeing Alixa standing behind him, her tanned arms hanging straight at her sides. She wore a loose, flowing robe of pale blue. The faint light flowing out of her half-open cabin door silhouetted her body inside the semi-transparent gown: long legs tapering to curving hips and a narrow waist, full, high breasts half exposed by the low neck of the robe, level shoulders that were wide for a woman. It was a body that sang songs of power and grace, beauty and softness.

It had an immediate effect on Blade, an effect which did not escape Alixa. She pointed toward the bulge in the front of his breeches and said softly, "Then it is not lack of manhood that has kept you away from me this past week? No, I see that. I did not really think so, either. So what keeps you back now? My father sleeps, and the captain cares little what guard is kept over us."

Blade started, suddenly aroused by more than desire for this lovely creature. Had she too noticed the captain's expressions? But she left him no time to ask. "Come, Master Blahyd. This may well be my last chance to taste a real *man*. There were few at Pelthros' court, and there will be none in Mardha. If we ever return from there I will be too old to find anyone to bed me except the jeweled fancymen who will bed with woman, man, ass, or dog for enough gold! Yes, Indhios means my father to remain in Mardha while he brews his plots. It will be long years before they ripen, and if they are carried through, my father and I may *never* return home. So come! Come give me some final bit of something clean and strong!"

She had raised her voice to a point where Blade found himself half expecting either sailors or the duke to awake. And she had raised her hands to the lacing of Blade's breeches and was stroking busily with her long, elegant fingers. Blade felt his breathing quicken. He realized that the woman beckoning him was no virgin. Or perhaps she merely had remarkable instincts about how to arouse a man—and a total lack of fear of the consequences.

He stepped forward and reached out both arms to seize her by the shoulders. She backed away towards her cabin door and opened it behind her. Blade followed her. In a moment they were inside and Blade reached behind him to close and bolt the door. Deftly she reached down and plucked his sword and dagger from their sheaths, then tossed them to the floor. They landed with a *thunk* on the thick rug. "Those will not be your weapons tonight, Master Blahyd," she said with a chuckle.

She shrugged the gown off her shoulders. It flowed

down onto the floor to lie in a pale blue pool around her ankles. Blade began stripping off his own gear and clothing. Only a fear of being overheard kept him from cursing loudly at balky straps and buckles. She stood silently before him, her hands at her sides again, until he was as naked as she. Before she could move, he stepped forward and pulled her against him until he could feel the high, firm breasts flattening against his chest. His hands rose up to her shoulders, then drifted down the exquisite curve of her spine to cup the small, firm buttocks and press her against him, until he heard in her breathing an arousal beginning to match his own.

He lifted her as lightly as he would a child and lowered her onto the bed, then stood looking down at her for a moment. She looked back at him, her gray eyes wide and blazing with her own desire. He lowered himself onto the bed, hands reaching out to cup the breasts now thrust towards him, to feel the delicate nipples harden against his palms, to draw his hands downward toward the blue-black furring of her mound and hear her gasp as he pressed down there.

She rolled toward him and he rolled toward her and entered. At the first moment he knew he had been right in his guess; this was no virgin. She accepted him smoothly and sheathed him snugly, milking him with muscles at first delicately controlled, then wilder and wilder in their motions as she was swept away by her own rising tide. Blade felt his control slipping too, and in the end they came together, she thrashing wildly and locking arms and legs around him as he poured himself into her.

It was such a totally absorbing act that Blade, who could and sometimes did keep going virtually all night, felt no immediate desire for a repetition. He lay beside her in comfortable satiation until a gentle knocking on the door made him jerk upright and snatch for his weapons.

"Hsst," came a soft voice from outside. "Brora here. If ye'd not be caught away from your guard post . . ." The sailor left the sentence unfinished, but Blade had no difficulty filling in the missing phrases. After hauling on a decent minimum of clothing, he turned back to the bed. Alixa stretched luxuriously and looked up at him.

"So soon?" She, obviously, was ready and willing to indulge in an all night bout.

"I'm afraid so."

"You *do* wield a weapon mightier than your steels." She wriggled all over at the memories. "Then go and take my gratitude if you can't take anything else for the moment. You have given me some powerful memories to take with me to Mardha."

Outside on the darkened deck Blade was very conscious of Brora's eyes on him. The sailor had a natural decency that kept him from making too many inquiries. But he did say, half to himself, "Ye be a lusty and a lucky man, by Druk."

Blade, even less willing to discuss the past hour, could only nod.

CHAPTER 6

Four more days passed. Blade heard the sailors telling each other that *Triumph* was now too far east as well as too far south for meeting pirates. But what if they happened to be out on a raid against the coast of Mardha? Pessimists who asked such questions were quickly hooted down. And perhaps they really were safe now. Blade noticed that the captain's face was now longer than ever before, while the Grand Duke and Alixa both seemed more cheerful than he had ever seen them.

There were no opportunities for him and Alixa to repeat their all-too-short encounter. Nor would there be one until Blade was on guard duty again or Alixa found some other safe occasion for letting him enter her cabin. The lady was lusty but not foolish. On the morning of the fifth day, Blade noticed her looking at him more intently than usual and repeatedly running her tongue across her lips. Perhaps she had found that occasion? He sensed she was about to step over toward him and perhaps speak when the lookout at the main top cut loose with a wild scream.

"Sail ho! Off the port beam! It's Neralers!"

The ship began to churn like a kicked anthill. Blade threw Alixa a wave of his hand as he dashed away in search of his armor and weapons. The few members of the duke's household on deck ran screaming below. The rest of the guard came charging up from their quarters, pulling on helms, cuirasses, leggings, and belts glittering with weapons. Behind them came the off-watch sailors, less well-equipped but even more ferocious looking with great shaggy beards spreading over bare chests and cutlasses heavy enough to behead an ox flashing in their massive hands. The sailors on watch darted below for their own weapons or opened the arms chests racked fore and aft and began handing out pikes and crossbows.

Steam hissed up from the galley stack as the cooks doused the galley fires. Younger sailors, limber as monkeys, swarmed up the ratlines with bows in their hands to take sharpshooting stations in the tops. At the very stern, Blade saw the captain talking urgently to the bosun, who then disappeared below to supervise the tiller crew. Blade would have given a good deal to hear what the captain said.

But he had no time to wonder, because the Neralers were coming up fast. With oars and their tall lanteen sails both working, they were rapidly closing in. It would be a straight, bitter fight against odds that lengthened moment by moment as more and more pirate ships rose over the horizon. Finally there were nine of them, all racing toward *Triumph*.

Blade knew resistance would have been hopeless against such odds except for the high, thick sides of *Triumph* and the pirates' own notorious lack of discipline. They tended to come dashing individually, devil take the hindmost, each seeking the greatest share of the glory and the booty for himself. Even so, beating off nine successive attacks by nearly two hundred pirates at a time was going to be a chancy thing at best.

He was fully armed now. As he stood at the railing

38

watching the nearest of the pirate ships race towards them, foam creaming at her ram bow, he felt a hand on his arm. He turned and saw Alixa. She was dressed in a dark blue robe, with a wide belt of red leather, and her neck, ears, and fingers sparkled with jewels. Blade was too stunned at the spectacle to speak for a moment. Instead he merely pointed.

She smiled grimly. "If we are taken, the Neralers will slaughter, enslave, or enlist all of us, except those who show they are worth holding for ransom." She raised her beringed hands. "These are my safe conduct, my proof that I am a great lady with great relatives who can pay a great ranson. Blood-mad pirates might not believe my words, but they will believe these."

"You show great courage," said Blade, with open respect in his voice. He had suspected that she would be no hysterical, sniveling girl in this crisis, but he was glad to have his guess confirmed.

"I am the daughter of a Grand Duke of Royth," she said simply. "And of a brave and honest man, which is fully as important. I do not want to disgrace him." She turned away to look at the approaching ships for a moment, then turned back and said more quietly, "If they take us, you will be my betrothed."

Blade managed to avoid gaping idiotically at the words. "Your betrothed? Why?"

"Fool!" she said the word with a laugh that took some of the harshness out of it. "To be betrothed to the daughter of a Grand Duke of mighty Royth, one must be a man of high station somewhere. If they think you such, the pirates will hold you for ransom along with me."

"Very true." Privately, Blade suspected that if the ship was taken, his chances of living long enough for the pirates to have anything to do about him except throw his body over the side were rather slim. Then shouts from all around him snapped his attention back to the pirates.

All nine ships were now within long bowshot. But instead of charging in to the attack in ones or twos, they were forming into a single line ahead, a line arrayed with professional skill. Blade heard the shouts give way to uneasy mutterings and curses as the sailors realized their main advantage was gone. None knew how.

Khystros appeared at Blade's right hand and ordered his daughter below. When she had gone he said softly, "There's planning behind this. And gold. Enough gold to make nine Neral pirate captains sacrifice their chances of glory and loot to make a more effective assault. Their paymaster wants a thorough job, it seems. Well, we shall see that they have to work to earn that gold." He turned on his heel and strode aft, a grim figure in his black plate armor with a well-battered broadsword swinging from his belt.

The pirates were now furling their sails, relying on oars alone as their line forged slowly around to head off *Triumph*. Blade could easily read their plan: get ahead of the ship, form a semicircle, and then come in against her from nine points on a full hundred and eighty degree arc. With their ability to move independently of the wind, they could easily close and then rely on their superior numbers to do the rest in hand-to-hand combat. The only chance *Triumph* had was to keep moving. Blade guessed that was what Khystros had gone aft to discuss with the captain.

By the time Khystros returned, to mount the short ladder to the foc'sle deck and turn to face the men assembled on deck, the pirates had formed their semi-circle. Then, as Khystros drew his sword and raised it over his head with a single graceful and defiant gesture, the tiller went hard over.

There was a moment's stunned silence; then as the turn continued and the deck began to heel, there was an uproar of curses, shouts, and clatters as men were thrown off their feet by the sudden angle of the deck. Blade knew enough about ships to realize that if this continued the ship would be taken aback. The wind would blow the sails back against the masts, they would tear themselves to shreds and the ship would be a helpless, immobile victim for the pirates. And he knew who was responsible for the turn.

He stormed aft, snatching his sword and dagger free as he ran. He burst down the ladder and into the tiller flat

40

with his weapons drawn, catching the captain leaning negligently against a beam, watching the tiller crew as they struggled to force the tiller hard over and keep it there. The captain had barely time to lower one hand towards his own sword when Blade's weapon came whistling down in a mightly slash. The captain's head jumped from his shoulders in a flurry of blood and sailed clear over the dumbfounded tiller crew. Blade shouted at them, "Put the tiller back over. PUT IT OVER! The captain was a traitor! That turn he ordered took us aback. The pirates are all around us." His manner and tone had their effect. As he charged back up the ladder to the deck he saw the sweating men strain at the tiller, bringing it back over.

But when he reached the deck, he saw that it was too late for any more maneuvering. Forwards and aft *Triumph* towered high above the decks of the pirate galleys, but amidships she was low enough so that an agile man might swarm up a rope onto her deck. Four of the pirate ships—two on either side—had slipped in. Grapnel hooks flew from them, to hook over railings and bits and provide passage for climbing men. Blade saw one hook snag a sailor and whip him over the side before he could even scream. And the pirate ships also had archers aboard, who were pouring arrows into the whole length of *Triumph*, so that no man could safely venture out on deck to cut the grapnel lines.

Arrows hissed and whistled about Blade as he dashed forward nonetheless, toward where the duke stood on the foc'sle deck, surrounded by his other guards. Miraculously, he made the trip unscathed, scrambled up the ladder, and shouted to the duke over the swelling battle roar, "The captain's dead. He gave the order to put the helm over."

"So he *was* a traitor. Thank you, Master Blahyd. I shall have—"

"Look out!" yelled Blade. Too late, he noticed half a dozen shaggy or bald heads appear over the foc'sle railing. A crossbow went *spung* and the duke went rigid, hands going up to his blood-spouting throat to clutch at the crossbow bolt rammed through it. For a moment he stood there, long enough for his men to turn, gape and groan; then he toppled to the deck with a metallic crash of armor. For another moment he kicked wildly, then was still.

Blade was too busy to worry about what effect the duke's fall might have on the minds of the men. The pirate with the crossbow had his own throat laid open by Blade's back-handed slash in a split second. The man beside him screamed as Blade smashed the sword pommel into his face; he lost his grip on the railing and toppled into the sea. A third man had time for one wild stroke of his own before Blade's riposte chopped through his arm and halfway through his body.

The other three hung back, momentarily too terrified of the blood-spattered giant confronting them. But Blade had no shortage of opponents. The pirates were swarming onto *Triumph's* deck by the dozens, clambering from their own ships across the decks of the ones already grapneled fast and pouring up the ropes. The ship's crew, unnerved by the duke's fall, were falling back or simply falling, under sword, cutlass, and axe. The pirate archers had ceased fire out of fear of hitting their own men, and the waist of *Triumph* was now a cauldron of clanging, flailing steel.

Battle madness was on Blade, and he hurled himself into the fighting with no thought beyond taking as many of the pirates with him as possible. He leaped from the foc'sle deck like a panther, landing on two unsuspecting pirates and smashing them to the deck with his massive weight. Before they could recover and try to rise, he had sworded one, daggered the other.

Aft, a man nearly as tall as Blade and even broader stood by the door to the cabins. He wore only ragged black trousers and a grimy once-white rag tied about his unkempt blond head. In his left hand swung a cutlass looking heavy enough to hew through iron bars. Like Brora, he had the air of a rough but deadly leader of even rougher and deadlier men.

Blade charged, his sword weaving a shimmering web in front of him as he tore through the press of struggling men like a mad bull splintering a rail fence. Out of the

42

corner of his eye he noticed Brora backed against a railing but keeping three pirates at bay with his whirling cutlass. Then he was on the big pirate, who barely had time to bring his cutlass up to guard against Blade's first stroke.

Heavy as the cutlass was, the big pirate could wield it more than fast enough. The first return stroke whistled past Blade's ear and by a finger's width missed splitting him from shoulder to groin. His return stroke clanged off the cutlass blade with a sound like a dropped anvil. Then they were at it hard and fast, with a steady crash of blades and stamping of feet.

Gradually, Blade became aware that the battle uproar behind them had faded. As the pirate stepped back for a moment, he took a split-second glance to either side. The deck was almost clear of the defenders—at least living ones—and most of the pirates were now standing and gaping at the duel of giants.

It was becoming a duel of weary giants now. Blade felt his joints beginning to creak and his muscles turning to the consistency of oatmeal. But he was utterly determined to hold on as long as the pirate chief and enough longer to drive his sword through the man's heart. Gradually, he began to realize that the pirate, strong as he was, was tiring even faster. The cutlass no longer lashed out to whistle about Blade's head. Instead it darted back and forth, parrying Blade's sword strokes. Blade knew that the combat was approaching its crisis. In a little more time the pirate would realize that the only thing left for him was to take his opponent with him. Blade knew that in that moment he would face a charge that he would have trouble meeting.

Without a pause, he switched in mid-stroke to a thrust, and saw his sword drive through the pirate's defenses and the point leave a red line across the man's shoulder before the descending cutlass smashed down again. Blade backed away for a moment, noting that the pirate was too weary to follow him, but stood gasping, as if rooted to the deck.

Then Blade came in again, whipping his sword into one thrust after another as fast as his fading arm muscles could move, seeing trickles of red emerge in one place af-

43

ter another. He saw a light beginning to glow in the pirate's eyes, too, and his chest heave as he gathered his last strength for the charge. The cutlass swung up into a guard position, then whistled down and rasped in a spray of sparks along Blade's sword. The force of the blow almost numbed Blade's hand. It was entirely a reflex action that raised the sword, then swung the point out at the exact moment the pirate chief lunged forward. Blade's point drove straight into his chest, so fast and so hard that the guard was brought up with a thud against the ribs. Then there was another much louder thud as the pirate toppled.

Blade was very close to joining him on the deck too. Only by staggering forward and pressing his hands against the bulkhead did he keep from falling on his face. When the fogginess had passed, he looked up and out, at the crowd of pirates amidships.

None of them were raising a weapon except the three who had their cutlasses pointed at Brora's chest. The look in their eyes as they watched Blade was something between surprise and respect. Then one of them, a lean and wiry little man, stepped forward and said loudly, so that all could hear:

"By the Law of the Brotherhood, you who have slain in fair and equal combat Oshawal Rida's son, a full Brother and Captain, may ask the right to join the Brotherhood and take Oshawal's place."

Before Blade could decide how to answer, there was a scream from behind him. The door to his left flew open with a crash and two pirates dragged a half-naked Alixa out onto the deck. The other pirates stared, and Blade saw eyes open and tongues drawn across lips. Before anyone else could move or speak, he stepped forward and placed his sword across Alixa's shoulders.

"Hold!" he roared. "If I am worthy to join your Brotherhood, then I claim protection for this lady, my betrothed, and for that man with the swords at his throat, my sworn comrade. Accept them also, or start guessing how many of you will die before I am slain!"

There were black looks of frustrated lust in Blade's direction. Somebody growled, "They said the daughter too,"

44

before somebody else snarled, "Shut up, you loose-jawed fool!" Blade took a firm grip on his sword, prepared to first give Alixa a quick death, then sell his own life at the expense of as many pirates as possible.

The small man raised a hand, and the mutterings died away. "It is not writ so in the Law of the Brotherhood. But for such a fighting man as you seem, the Law can be—eh, *bent*, I daresay. Silence!" to the men behind him. "Those words of the Law were to give us good fighting men. Any of you yapping dogs who think this be not a good fighting man, step forward and best him as he bested Oshawal. Then I'll own you true and rightful chief." The silence finally came. "Then so be it." He stepped forward and stretched out both hands to take Blade's.

CHAPTER 7

That evening Blade stood at the railing of the late Oshawal's galley, *Thunderbolt,* and watched the flames roar up from *Triumph.* To one side of him at a discreet distance stood Alixa and a little beyond her Brora, and to the other side stood Oshawal's first mate, the wiry little pirate who had offered Blade entrance into the Brotherhood. His name was Tuabir.

Blade was contemplating the road by which he had traveled to his new status as a pirate of Neral, or at least a candidate for the status. It was a precarious position, but almost certainly better than waiting around as a high-ranking prisoner until it was discovered that no ransom would ever be forthcoming for him. And he had made it less precarious than it might have been by a stroke of practical leadership.

In answer to the grumbling among Oshawal's men about taking an ignorant fighter, perhaps a landlubber, as captain, Blade had climbed on the railing and spoken to them.

"Oshawal Rida's son was a mighty warrior whose

45

prowess will be sung for centuries. And he was also a wise man in the ways of the sea. Before I am worthy to step into hs shoes, I must gain some small part of that same wisdom. When we reach Neral, I shall ask some worthy Brother and Captain to take me on as mate and teach me the ways of the sea. When I have learned enough, I shall return to take my place aboard *Thunderbolt*. Until then, follow Tuabir. I will not lead brave men into danger through not knowing the ways of the sea." In the wake of that speech, the grumblings turned to cheers, the black looks faded, and he caught sight of Tuabir nodding and grinning.

Of his two companions, the realistic Alixa, grief-stricken as she was for her dead father, had yet accepted Blade's stratagem with a shrug of her graceful shoulders. Blade, after all, had used a ruse much like what she herself had planned. Moreover, she admitted that it was one that would quite possibly offer them both a much better chance of safety than hers. Still, he did not venture to approach her or speak to her that evening as she stood by the rail of *Thunderbolt*, wrapped in her blue cloak and watching the flames roar up from *Triumph* in an eye-searing pyramid.

Brora, on the other hand, had nearly thrown himself overboard rather than accept the protection of someone who had turned traitor to all honest seamen by joining the pirates. Blade was even less willing to approach the tough sailor that evening. He knew Brora would have preferred to be, if not a corpse burning in the flames, at least one of the shackled slaves in the lower benches and holds of *Thunderbolt* and her sister vessels. Blade knew that only learning he had joined the pirates with the intention of escaping as soon as possible would make Brora respect him again. But that intention was something he would have to keep secret for some time to come and pay whatever price might be necessary.

Certainly he had no idea of how it might be accomplished, the morning after the burning of the ship, when a sea flecked with whitecaps tossed burned timbers about. Even Indhios' gold could not keep a fleet of Neraler pirates together beyond the moment of victory. The fleet was breaking up. Those ships that had lost too many men for safe navigation or further fighting began the long beat to the northwest, homeward bound for Neral. Those still strong enough for further raiding or with crews greedy for more loot turned the opposite way, to spread out along the shipping lanes in search of their next prey.

With her captain and fifteen of her men dead, *Thunderbolt* was one of those that turned for home. Day darkened into night, which in turn faded into day, and so it continued for seventeen days and nights. Although the lateen-rigged *Thunderbolt* could sail closer to the wind than any square-rigger, it was still a long beat. On more than one occasion Tuabir abandoned hope of making any progress against the contrary winds. Then the drums beat the crew and the slaves to man the sixty oars and pounded out the cadence that kept those oars moving until the winds blew right again. And on one occasion they had to furl the sails, batten down oarports and hatches, and run helpless as a canoe shooting rapids before a howling northwest gale that blew for two days.

It was during that gale that Alixa decided to make the best of the fact that she and Blade would be much in each other's company for a long time, and there would be none to judge what they did except the rough and bawdy pirates. Blade realized they would wonder if a lusty man betrothed to such a magnificent specimen of female did not indulge himself as often as possible. Nor did he really disagree with Alixa's notion that there was no point in observing the proprieties conjured up by the dessicated chaperones of an over-civilized court. He had always been a man to take his pleasures as lustily and as frequently as possible. So Alixa spent most of those two nights and others afterwards in Blade's bed, and by no means all of that time was spent sleeping.

They had eleven days of voyaging after the storm blew itself out, eleven days of fair skies, cooperative winds, and seas sometimes whitecapped but never wild.

On the evening of the seventeenth day just before sunset the lookout called down, "Land ho." An hour later

47

Blade on deck saw the line of the horizon that was Neral. Tuabir told him that it was customary to lie off until morning unless one was being pursued and not enter the harbor by night. When morning came and Blade, after a bout with Alixa and a refreshing sleep afterwards, came on deck, he saw why. And he also saw why Neral had never been taken or even seriously threatened since the Brotherhood had made it their base some hundred or more years before.

The island was a natural fortress further improved by human ingenuity. It stretched away some forty miles to the north. But it was the south end, the one they were approaching, that was the heart of its strength. The entire southern end of the island was sheer cliff more than two hundred feet high, fringed with reefs extending out two or three miles. All, that is, except for one channel leading to an equally narrow slash in the cliffs. Behind that narrow slash, half a mile long but no more than a hundred feet wide at most, lay an immense landlocked harbor, large enough to accommodate three times the Brotherhood's two hundred ships. Climbing up the steep sides of that harbor were all the buildings that housed the Brotherhood and all the activities needed to sustain their power. Looming over fleet, harbor, and town alike was the vast gray bulk, visible fifty miles away on a clear day, called only the Mountain. It separated the southern portion of the island from the northern. Over winding, easily blocked paths the meat, grain, and garden stuffs from the farms and herds that filled the northern portion of the island came in to feed the Brotherhood and fill its storerooms. Those storerooms, Tuabir said, never held less than a year's ample rations. The Brotherhood could loll in comfort in its fortress and sneer at any opponent for far longer than that opponent could keep a fleet near or an army on the island. They had in fact done so three times.

Tuabir ordered the sails furled and the masts lowered into their cradles amidships. The rowers manned their benches, and the drums began to beat a slow, creeping cadence. *Thunderbolt* was just approaching the entrance to the channel, marked by two squat buoys with glass oil lanterns mounted on them, when a red flag went up on a pole jutting out from the cliff to the left of the passage through the rock.

Tuabir cursed. "Another ship coming out," he muttered. "Back your oars!" he yelled. *Thunderbolt* crabbed her way clear of the channel and waited. Soon the boom of an oarmaster's drum and the thump of oars came to their ears, echoing off the high walls of the passage; then a ship came in sight. Tuabir grinned when he saw the bow emblem—a stylized female figure, green and surrounded by flowing black robes.

"Sister Cayla's *Sea Witch*. Coming out to exercise her rowers after refit, no doubt. Aye, there's a lusty lady. And you'd best take her for the fighter and captain she is, if you want to keep those cods you've been keeping so busy. I've seen her duel a man half again her size and slice him up until he was as well-gelded as any cony. She'll not find much happiness in learning we've taken Khystros and all his while Witch was hove down for a bottom-clean."

Sea Witch was a small galley, rowing only twenty oars a side, low-built and almost bare of ornamentation. As she came abeam of *Thunderbolt* the oars slapped down into the water to lie there while the crew ran smartly to winch the masts into their sockets. A small figure in green popped out of a hatch aft and strode forward through the men. They gave way to either side as the figure passed up to the bow and hailed *Thunderbolt*.

Somehow, Blade had been expecting that any woman who could captain her own ship among the crowd of professional tough customers that was the Brotherhood would be large, tough, and disagreeably unfeminine. Instead, the lethal Sister/Captain Cayla was visibly at least half a head shorter than most of her crew. She wore a trim green tunic-and-breeches outfit with black leather belt and boots that would have carried a fifty-guinea price tag in any Chelsea boutique. Face and figure were at least presentable, as far as Blade could tell across fifty yards of water, while her close-cropped blonde hair shimmered in the sun like a cap of gold. Her voice as it came across that gap was roughened by many years of shouting above battle and storm but no worse than Blade had heard from ticket takers on a score of London buses.

"Hoy, Tuabir! Back so soon? Pickings that slim where you went?" Tuabir stiffened at the mocking note in her voice.

"Good pickings indeed. We were of those who fell in with Grand Duke Khystros and all his. You know the reward promised for that?"

"Wha—?"

"Aye. We took his ship. The Grand Duke, or what the fire left of him, is down among the fishes now." Tuabir gestured over the side.

Cayla turned in an instant from fashion plate to fishwife. The stream of curses that poured out of her mouth and spattered about the ears of those aboard *Thunderbolt* would have made any sergeant-major turn green with envy.

Finally she ran out of curses, or more likely out of breath, and shouted, "All right, you bastards. You made sure I wouldn't get any part in this! You didn't want to let me have any more reputation, so I could be a threat to you and the other big boys!" She paused again, then, sharply:

"Where's Oshawal?"

Tuabir shook his head and jerked his thumb over the side in another down-with-the-fishes gesture. "Dead. You see beside me the one who killed him. And he wouldn't take Oshawal's place, because he said he would be leading a crew into danger through not knowing our seas. He wants a chance to serve as a mate before taking *Thunderbolt* out on his own. Aye, his head's as good as his arm, and his arm's a thing like you've never seen."

"Indeed." The interest in Cayla's voice sounded clearly. Blade wished the two ships were close enough for him to see the expression on her face. But Cayla had apparently seen and heard enough. She barked an order, and the crew scrambled back to the oars, which began their steady beat again, carrying *Sea Witch* out to where the wind could fill her sails.

As the other ship pulled away, Tuabir turned to Blade

and said softly, "Master Blahyd, I think she has her eye on you. As for me, I'd be happier with a sea adder having its eye on me."

Cayla's own word seemed a reasonable answer. "Indeed?"

"Aye. She has ambitions beyond being a mere Captain. She would sit on the Captain's Council of the Brotherhood. And what she would do then, Druk alone knows. It's said she was once a Serpent Priestess in Mardha and would still see the Serpent Cult rising on all shores of Ocean."

Alixa came out in time to hear Tuabir's last words and stare after the departing *Sea Witch*. The pirate looked at her, drew Blade farther off to one side, and muttered to him in an even lower voice than before, "Take care for your lady. I don't know what she is to you in truth, whether your betrothed or not. And I care little. But if Cayla has her eye on you and sees another woman standing in her way, the lady'll have great need of prayers, for nothing else will help her. Among the Free Women of the Brotherhood there's the Woman's Duel when two desire the same man, and it's to the death. Cayla fights with a dagger and a little whip no longer than your arm. But I puked myself empty for a day and a night after seeing what she did with them the last time she fought, and I wasn't the only one. Had you but passed the lady off as your sister, she'd be ten times safer. Cayla'd stand beside you to defend her from insult then. But as it is . . ." Tuabir shrugged.

Blade shrugged too, a gesture far from reflecting his true feelings. To become involved with yet another woman, and this one a sadistic she-pirate with vast and nameless ambitions, would weaken even further the tightrope on which he was going to have to walk for a painfully long time. He hoped Tuabir was mistaken, but his own reading of Cayla's voice left him little hope of that.

However, for the moment there were other things to think of. The oarmaster began his drum beat, the oars swung forward and splashed down, and *Thunderbolt* surged forward up the channel towards the gap in the rocks. As they passed the entrance and slipped into the shadow, Blade noticed that the rock on either side showed signs of extensive working. Railed galleries and slits had been carved at several levels on both sides, from just above the water to nearly a hundred feet up. Blade guessed that from those galleries and slits arrows, stones, burning oil, and many other sorts of nastiness could be hurled down on any ships foolish enough to try breaking into the Brotherhood's fortress through the channel.

Farther on, they came to a broad ledge, partly natural but also extended by more carving. On it were piled a score or more of enormous logs, blackened with tar and grease, and coils of rope as thick as a man. There was yet another barrier for the passage—an enormous boom that could be easily fastened in place in any emergency, to rip out the bottom of any ship.

Blade tried to calculate the amount of work that must have been involved in all the excavations from the living rock he had seen. He found himself appalled at his most conservative estimate. No wonder the pirates had an insatiable demand for slaves, and no wonder the slaves died like flies! The more he saw of the fortifications of Neral, the more he realized how justified the pirates were in their casually arrogant assumption that the island was impregnable. And, more personally, the more he realized how difficult making his own escape would be when the time came. Possibly getting out of the channel would be easier than getting in, but he doubted it.

Thunderbolt crept up the passage. The thump and splash of the slowly moving oars echoed from the looming gray walls. Blade shivered in the chill shadows and wrapped his cloak more tightly about him. Finally they glided out into the sunlit inner basin. Blade looked up at the heart of the Brotherhood's fortress rising all about him.

Although he had looked at the symbol-crowded map of the area many times, Blade was still awed by the scale of the whole thing now that he saw it in reality. At the water's edge docks and piers jutted out into the harbor, some of them covered, enough of them to accommodate four hundred ships. Just above them lay the building ways and their auxiliaries—the storage sheds for timber, masts, rope, metalwork, and everything else needed to build ships. Mixed in with them were the storehouses for loot, the barracks for the dockyard and rowing slaves, their rank smell drifting across even the miles of water to attack Blade's nose, and the forges and foundries puffing up their clouds of black smoke. On a terrace farther up the slope stood the shops, taverns, gaily painted brothels, and the living quarters for the free sailors and the servants. Higher still were the homes of shopkeepers and mates, and highest of all, surrounded by its own walls and served by its own shops was the street of the Captains, the rulers of the Brotherhood.

From the water's edge to the uppermost of the Captains' stout brick homes the slope stretched more than a mile and rose five hundred feet in that mile. Beyond the houses another wall studded with towers wrapped itself around the whole base, and beyond that rose the frowning peak of the Mountain. Not only did this base represent an incredible amount of labor, it also represented incredible wealth. Blade could easily see why the Neralers had bled the Four Kingdoms white for a century, where the wealth had gone—and how the masters of such a fortress might begin to think of becoming masters of a Kingdom.

There was a sudden flurry of running figures all up and down the slopes as *Thunderbolt* slid across the basin toward her dock. At Blade's side Tuabir grinned. "So we are indeed the first back from all the fleet that took the duke. I thought that, from what Cayla said, but it was almost too much to hope."

On the roof of one of the covered docks somebody stood now, frenziedly going through a complicated series of passes with a pair of orange and black signal flags. Tuabir barked an order, and a sailor sprang up onto *Thunderbolt's* prow and set a similar pair dancing. A moment's pause ashore, and then cheers that spread like a fire around the basin and up the slope until it seemed the whole vast bowl was ringing with them. From two stout, high red brick towers of a building on the Captains' street yellow smoke began to stream up into the sky in a sinuous cloud.

"Eh, the call to Festival!" said Tuabir with another grin. "And few of the fleet will be home to share the wine, the women, and the joy. Have you a stout head as well as a stout arm, Master Blahyd? You'll truly be needing it tonight for a Festival of the Brotherhood."

Blade nodded absently. Festival—some sort of massive celebration? It would be one way of getting a chance to look around him, meet people, get a better impression of this colossal den of thieves which had sucked him in. But he would rather have had a chance to be alone and think out his next move.

He was utterly certain by now that Khystros' assumptions about a pirate conspiracy were absolutely right, and he was more than inclined to believe the duke's suspicions about the Chancellor as well. He had heard too much over the past eighteen days, and now these cheers were one more piece of evidence. Fighting and intriguing. In every world, it seemed he sooner or later wound up doing one or both.

CHAPTER 8

Tuabir armed four of his toughest sailors to the teeth and escorted Blade, Brora, and Alixa up to a house on the Captains' street. Like its neighbor, from which the Festival signal was still streaming, it had two high towers with slit-narrow windows. It was into a room high up in one of these towers that Tuabir led his charges, up a winding circular staircase. Although the room was comfortable and well heated, there was a certain austerity about it that made Blade ask if he and his companions were guests, prisoners, or something in between.

"Say that you are prisoners for the time of Festival, so you'll still be living when it's over," replied Tuabir. "No Free Woman and no man not prepared for a fight goes out beyond locked doors tonight. And for you three, not yet initiated into any status among the Brotherhood . . ." The sailor shrugged. "The Master Blahyd may well go out with proper care, being a well-set-up fighting man even if not yet known as such. But even he would do well to wear a Candidate's belt." He pulled out of his pouch a length of blue and gold cloth and handed it to Blade. "That shows you be Free but not Initiated. You can neither challenge nor be challenged to duel."

After a moment's hesitation Blade tied the belt around his waist. He intensely disliked going out and relying on anything but his own strength and skill. But he had to get out and look around before he could do any planning for anything. And it was too soon to get caught up in any more fights, not if his status was so uncertain.

After removing all of his weapons except a sheathed dagger in his belt for eating and another knife concealed in his boot top, Blade turned to Brora and Tuabir. "I call you both friends now. May I ask you, as friends, to take care that nothing happens to the Lady Alixa?"

Brora nodded and looked hard at Tuabir, who also nodded after a moment. During the nearly three weeks of the voyage to Neral, Blade had seen something far short of friendship but close to mutual respect growing up between the two tough sailors. Each saw that the other was a man who could handle a ship and a crew nearly as well as himself, and neither could quite bring himself to wholly reject such a man. So Blade knew that he had at least two friends to guard his back as he went out to sample the Festival.

He found that he needed more than a hard head to get through the Festival. He needed a strong stomach also. And even with both of these, he found it beyond him to enjoy the Festival.

Tuabir, as bloody-handed as any other pirate of long standing, still had considerable decency and self control. And while at sea on a raid the pirates had been as tough and well disciplined as any crew of fighting seamen who want to die in bed must be. But now, safe on shore and with money in their pockets and a victory to celebrate, the pirates ran wild. After a few hours of watching their notions of amusement, Blade knew he would have to get free of Neral as soon as possible before his own revulsion caused him to make some slip that would sign his death warrant. And he also knew he was willing to spend as much time here in this Dimension as might be needed to defeat the pirates' plans to seize the Kingdom of Royth. The idea of any civilized country in the hands of the pirates made Blade's stomach turn.

There was only a pale glow on the western horizon when he went out. But the light from the torches spluttering in brackets on the walls of the taverns and brothels made the streets noon-bright. There were sentries patrolling the streets in ominous groups of four. The sentries cast sharp looks at Blade's size and other looks at his belt but left him alone. Otherwise, everybody was too intent on his own pleasures to pay much attention to the huge newcomer striding along among them and trying not to look disgusted.

There was a House of Dreams. Blade was practically dragged inside it by two burly doormen who bellowed in his ear, "All the dreams Druk can send for only five silver bits! Come, worthy sir, come seek our dreams!" Inside some forty men and women were sitting on padded quilts spread across the stone floor, breathing in blue smoke rising from glazed bowls. As he watched, he saw one of the men turn slowly around, stare at one of the women, then fall backwards on to his quilt and curl up like a dog, knocking over his bowl. It spilled a smoldering dark blue-black powder out onto the floor. A slave attendant rushed across and hastily swept up the powder with a brush.

Blade backed out hastily. Even after only a few whiffs of the blue smoke, he found his head swimming and his eyes peculiarly sensitive to the light. He wondered briefly if the powder was addictive as he brushed past the doormen and headed farther down the streets.

There was a House of Whips. From inside it sounded wild screams of delight and other screams of pain. Blade nerved himself to step inside. He was rewarded by the

56

spectacle of two women dancing, or trying to dance, nude in a sand pit while four brawny attendants sent long lashes tipped with metal slicing over their heads, about their feet, and occasionally into their flesh. They must have been dancing for hours already. Their hair was matted with sweat and their bodies were glazed with sweat, oil, and blood from half a dozen open whip cuts. A man beside Blade muttered, without taking his eyes off the dancers, "They think they will be allowed to go afterwards. But they are to be killed in honor of the Festival. Wait and see that big fellow in the black tights lay on the kill-whip." Blade swallowed hard and left the House of Whips even faster than he had left the House of Dreams. The pirates, it seemed, were addicted—in mind if not body—to sadism, drugs, everything ugly. Blade wondered if this were deliberate policy on the part of their leaders, who were unwilling to rely on a freely given loyalty and instead chose to manipulate their men in this gruesome fashion.

There were women wrestling naked in tubs of mud or copulating with men on stages. There were other dream places, with the drugs in liquid form rather than in smoking powders. There were strip shows, although Blade wondered how something so comparatively mild could compete with the more exotic amusements elsewhere on the street. There were bars and brothels, and inevitably there were wandering drunks and prowling whores.

Blade saw one of the drunks solicit one of the whores. When she pushed him away and he staggered over against the wall and sat down, his companion whipped out a razor-edged knife and slashed the girl's cheek open from hairline to jawline. Blade's control snapped then. He came up behind the knifewielder and chopped him across the back of the neck, pulling the blow just enough to avoid leaving a corpse lying in the street. With luck the man would never know that a Candidate had hit him, but Blade at this point hardly cared.

He turned to look for the girl, but she darted whimpering away into an alley so black and forbidding that even Blade for a moment hesitated to follow her. Then he plunged into the darkness, guided by the sound of running feet ahead. He would not leave the girl to crawl off like an animal into some corner and heal herself—or die of an infected wound—even if this was the custom of the pirates. He shuddered again at the thought of a civilized community fallen into the hands of the Neralers.

Suddenly he heard the footsteps ahead of him change direction, first bearing off to the right and then beginning to climb. He heard echoes, and knew the passage must lead into one of the tunnels that honeycombed the slope. The girl had turned into the tunnel. Should he follow? Before he could decide, he heard a rumble and felt a vibration in the cobblestoned floor of the alley under his feet. And before he could react to that, the cobblestones dropped out from under him and he plunged down into a blackness even more complete than that of the alley.

The fall was enough to knock the wind out of him, but a thick layer of quilts and cushions broke most of the impact. He sat up instantly, drawing his dagger. As he did so, a pale light suddenly flooded the chamber.

He was sitting in the bottom of a shaft some twenty feet deep and eight feet in diameter at the bottom. The cushions and quilts were made of a uniform dark green cloth glimmering with little sparkles in the light, which Blade saw came from a lantern behind a heavy glass panel set in the door of the shaft. The door itself was also green—old copper—and bare of ornament except for what first looked like a capital *W* in the middle. Then Blade saw that the *W* was made up of two pairs of black enameled serpents, their jewel-eyed heads together at the bottom. He felt a cold sinking in his stomach, remembering what Tuabir had said about Cayla's being a former Serpent Priestess of Mardha. And remembering that, he was not particularly surprised a moment later when the door slid noiselessly open and Cayla's voice said softly:

"Come to me, Blahyd."

Blade stepped through the door with his dagger firmly held ready to strike, and found himself in a tunnel sloping downward. The walls and ceiling were rough-hewn slimy rock, but the floor was tiled in smooth green and black

58

patterns through which stylized serpents writhed. Small lanterns in glass-fronted niches filled the tunnel with more of the same pallid light.

He stalked downward, prepared to follow the tunnel as far as it went, even into the foundations of the island. He was therefore a little surprised when it ended in a blank wall after less than fifty feet. Or at least it gave the appearance of a blank wall, because he had barely come to a stop before Cayla's voice came again, the same words in the same tone. The wall slid aside, and Blade stepped through, went down two shallow steps, and looked about him.

He was in a high-domed, circular chamber about fifty feet across, lit by more of the ubiquitous lanterns, these now hung from brackets set in the walls. The floor was the same uneasily familiar black and green serpent pattern. In the exact center of the chamber, on a dais raised some four feet off the floor, stood a stone altar in the form of a monstrous coiled serpent. Its head was toward Blade, and inside its gaping maw a small fire burned, sending coils of pungent green smoke up between the stabbing gilded fangs. Blade sniffed at the smoke, which hazed the chamber. It was not the same drug as the House of Dreams had offered. He had no time to wonder whether this was good or bad, because Cayla stepped out from behind the altar, uncoiling herself with a grace as sinuous as though she herself was a serpent.

She wore a green robe which covered her completely except for hands and face, a necklace of black stones, and a tiara of more black stones set in silver. Her face—and it was a strong and well-formed face, seen from close range—was totally expressionless.

"So you came, Blahyd?" Her voice, too, was almost expressionless, except for a slightly mocking note of inquiry.

He could not help asking in reply, "Did I have a choice?"

"You could have refused to follow that girl. But I knew you would not. Just as I know you are planning to desert us as soon as you can."

Blade would have found it convenient at that moment

to sink through the floor. He was as close as he had ever been to giving way to raw panic. He wondered if he were facing a telepath and suspected that coping with one would prove beyond him.

When he could get his tongue and lips into motion again, he could only say, "Why do you say that?"

"I am adept at reading the subtle messages of voice and face and stance, Master Blahyd. It is an art that can be acquired by proper training, just as the swordsmanship of which you seem so rightly proud."

Blade, after a moment of indulging his relief that nothing paranormal was working here, looked about the chamber again. "This is not the work of the pirates."

"No, nor of any man living. These swinish animals who crawl over the surface of the island and think they are burrowing deep into it know nothing of what lies inside. No more than lice know what lies inside a man."

"Indeed." It again seemed a useful enough word, when one absolutely had to say something.

"You fear me, Blahyd."

"I do. You are the unknown."

"Am I, Blahyd?" She stepped forward and he caught her musky scent. He was conscious that it was beginning to arouse him. "Are women unknown to you?"

"I have known many women."

"And you shall know one more." She reached back to undo the clasp of the necklace and laid it gently on the stone floor. She took the tiara off and laid it beside the necklace. Blade's arousal was now well past the beginning stage. She noticed it, and Blade could not help being gratified as her eyes wandered over him and widened noticeably. Then she stepped forward until she grasped his hands and lifted them to the collar of her robe. He found the small black metal catch there, fumbled for a moment, then undid it.

The robe fell away like the veil falling from a statue. As he had expected, she was nude under it. And she was superbly built, better than he had expected: without Alixa's grace, but trim, compact, well muscled. He lifted his hands to her small, firm breasts and stroked the pink

60

nipples with his thumbs, feeling the nipples bud and swell and hearing her gasp. Her own hands drifted lightly over his chest, playing with the hair, then down across his belly to flick gently his swollen phallus. His hands left her breasts and crept downward to play finger games in her blonde bush—a darker blonde than her gleaming, close-trimmed head and curly where the other grew straight. Again she gasped. Her hands rose to his shoulders, pressed down. She gave a little leap upwards and her supple legs wrapped themselves serpentlike (the idea gave Blade a momentary chill) around his massive torso. As her arms and legs pulled her against him, he drove into her and felt her shudder almost at once. It had been a long time since this one had had a man. He was determined to make sure that it would be a long time before she needed one again. It was the only way he could see to take away that maddening coolness and contempt and perhaps make her willing or able to tell more about her plans.

He was able to hold her clear of the floor as he continued his thrusting; she was light and his own strength seemed to peak. On and on he went, until he felt her body becoming slick with sweat and felt it dripping down his own. Still he kept on, hearing her begin to moan in protest, feeling her body writhe in his arms, until those arms themselves began to turn heavy and ache. Still he kept on, until her mouth opened to emit a sound that was more of a gurgle than anything else and her legs unlocked themselves by pure reflex. She would have fallen if he had not still kept his own aching arms around her.

It was not until he had placed her on the cushions in front of the altar that her eyes flickered open and once more stared expressionlessly into his. Blade found her continued detachment after such a bout a little frightening, but even more what she said.

"I have mated before the eyes of the Serpent. I could have done so years ago, but none of the pigs and sots among the pirates were worthy. None of them had a mind. But you—you—"

"What about me?"

"You are so eager to know what you must do! As eager as you were a few minutes ago. Well, you have pleased me so greatly in the mating that I shall tell you."

Blade was even more appalled by what he learned in the next few minutes than he had been by the Festival. The pirates at least limited themselves to human vices, however ugly. This—this female *thing*—had notions far beyond those.

She had indeed been a Serpent Priestess in Mardha, and was one still. The island of Neral had once been the great sacred place of the Serpent Cult, the school of its priestesses, the breeding place of the sacred serpents. This chamber was one of the uppermost of many, connected by miles of tunnels that did in fact plunge to the foundations of the island and below, all carved out over many, many centuries.

But the cult had fallen on lean days as its worshipers dropped away or were slain in the persecutions launched by all the Four Kingdoms. Finally, it had been decided by a secret conclave of the surviving priestesses to abandon Neral. They would keep the cult alive in smaller, less vulnerable centers all over the world.

But a hundred years ago, when the Brotherhood seized Neral and began making it their fortress, the Serpent Priestesses had decided to send some of their number among the pirates and see what might be done with them—or to them, if it came to that. For that hundred years, there had always been at least one Priestess among the Free Women of the Brotherhood, but only Cayla herself had ever risen to the rank of Captain, with all the influence and freedom that meant.

"And my influence will be yet greater if I take as my Companion a man such as you, Blahyd. If you can defeat Oshawal, there is no other Captain who could stand against you in a duel. And if you can learn the art of piracy as well as I suspect you can, you will soon have wealth and influence of your own. Together we can be a mighty power in the Brotherhood."

"And then?"

She was silent for a moment. "The Captain's Council

takes the gold of Chancellor Indhios of Royth and reaches out for the whole Kingdom. When they have it, however, they will not know what to do with it. You saw the Festival?" Blade nodded. "If the Brothers find themselves possessed of a whole Kingdom, they will glut themselves on women and dream dust and liquor and soon be unfit to rule an acre of onion patch. Then two strong people, who know their own minds and have a loyal following of good fighters *and* the aid of the conclaves of the Cult . . ." She did not need to finish. Blade nodded in understanding.

"Then it is resolved between us? You can rule a Kingdom with me, Blahyd! Would you reject that even if you could?"

Blade grinned wolfishly. "By that you mean I will never leave here alive if I do not agree with your plans?"

"Of course. Or perhaps you will die elsewhere, if I pass on word of your plans to escape. If we Priestesses had ever been soft, ten times over would the Cult have perished without a trace. But we have been strong, and so it lives. And when we have Royth at our feet, it will not only live, but rise again to glory!" Her voice rose to a pitch of exaltation, the first emotion he had heard from her all that night.

That was not the end of their conversation, for there were still practical details to be worked out. How Blade should swear allegiance to Cayla for his term as mate aboard *Sea Witch*. Whether he could bring Brora with him (Blade insisted, for he wanted his back protected if at all possible, and won his point). Much more. And then they made love again.

The noise and glare of Festival had died by the time Blade stood again on the surface. The streets were gray and silent in the early dawn, fit only for ghosts and people on such strange business as Blade himself. It occurred to him that not once had Cayla mentioned Alixa. Perhaps jealousy was one of the things she considered a softness? Perhaps. But he wished he could be more certain. He had learned that it was always a mistake to assume anything about a woman's jealousy.

CHAPTER 9

Cayla handled the little details of taking Blade on as her mate with a competence and a grasp of politics that impressed Blade in spite of himself. She sponsored him in his Initiation, when he stood up before the Captains' Council, let blood from a gash in his arm drip on to a small altar of Druk, the patron deity of seafarers, and said:

"By Druk, I swear to serve the Brotherhood, obey its laws in all ways, heed the word of the Council of Captains, shed my blood for it without stint as I do here, and hold my own life lightly if only the Brotherhood live. If I foreswear myself, may my Brothers turn away from me, my ship be swallowed up by Druk's green sea, and Druk himself cast me forth from his halls as foul and corrupt."

Cayla also sponsored the elevation of her former first mate to the rank of Captain, to make a vacancy for Blade—and also to earn the mate's gratitude. One more client among the Captains. When she hooked the jeweled dagger of his predecessor onto his belt, she said loudly, "Wear this and wield this as well as he who wore it before you," and Blade saw the other man almost glowing with pride. He also saw Alixa glowering at him, and afterwards she rejected all explanations and stamped away in a rage. He sighed, shrugged, and told Tuabir to continue his watch over Alixa.

"Aye, that I will do. The more for her sake than for yours, now. What can that witch have done to you, that you rush off to join her for mate—or mating?" It occurred to Blade that while Tuabir might not be adept like Cayla, he had a sharp eye and a fear of no man, woman, or beast. He might not be able to keep the old pirate as a friend now, but it would be wise not to make him into an enemy.

Then, quickly, there was too much for Blade to do to

leave him with time for any worrying about his own intrigues or those of anybody else. *Sea Witch* had already been refitted and supplied for her next raiding voyage, and Cayla was anxious to be out and away again as soon as possible. But she would not leave until she was satisfied that Blade knew the ship and how to handle her and her crew as well as possible—or at least, as well as possible after ten days of instruction.

Blade spent every one of those ten days aboard *Sea Witch*, poring over charts and lists and navigational instruments, exploring every part of the ship from the masthead to the bilge, and finally standing aft beside Cayla as she watched him put the crew through every possible maneuver and exercise, flaying him at the top of her voice if he made a mistake. At times, being Cayla's first mate felt like being back at officer-training school, being tongue-lashed by the drill sergeants. But her competence as a sailor, like her political judgment, was something he had to respect. Cayla was now a friend, and it would be sheer suicide to make her into an enemy.

Finally, at the end of the eleventh day, she admitted him to her bed again, and as they lay in delicious exhaustion afterwards she told him of her plans for the voyage. It was a daring scheme she had in mind, and the risks of disaster were great, but the rewards of success would be even greater.

The County of Tram lay near the northern end of the coast of Mardha. It was almost an island, about sixty miles by thirty, and connected to the coast by a long isthmus no more than two miles wide. To save coastal shipping the long and dangerous passage around the shores of the County, the Counts of Tram had built a canal through the isthmus, for which they charged a stiff toll. A fair-sized town had grown up around the canal. In addition, there were at this time of year seldom less than thirty ships waiting at either end of the canal for passage. And there was the money from the tolls, stored in small forts at either end also. There were few places in the Four Kingdoms where so much wealth was concentrated in such a small area.

Not that it was entirely ripe for the plucking. The counts maintained a fair-sized fleet of war galleys and armed merchant vessels to patrol their coasts and the approaches to the canal. Also, both the canal entrances and the town were fortified in a rather haphazard fashion. Any large fleet approaching would certainly be detected and engaged on the way in. And no single ship could carry enough fighters to face the garrisons.

But two or three ships might achieve surprise, particularly if they came in by night, skirting the northern and eastern coasts that were supposed to be too reef-strewn for safe navigation. Cayla knew passages through the reefs—she said they were marked in ancient charts drawn up by the Serpent Priestesses.

"And as for the rest—it is always easiest to take a fortress that has not been threatened for many years. Its defenders become lazy and their watchfulness fades, because they think they have no need to worry." Almost as an afterthought, she added, "The Counts of Tram were great in the persecution of our Cult. They stuffed their coffers with gold and jewels looted from our shrines, and they filled their dungeons and torture chambers with our priestesses and acolytes." There was a flare of vengeful rage in her eyes.

Esdros, the former first mate, was joining them with his new ship, *Spider Prince*. But they needed a third, if possible.

"What about Tuabir and *Thunderbolt*?" asked Blade. "He seems to be a tough fighter and a good captain. And *Thunderbolt*'s larger and has a bigger crew than either *Prince or Witch*."

"All that is true," said Cayla. "But I cannot help thinking that Tuabir is your friend and supporter more than mine."

"If I am your Companion, my friends and supporters are yours."

"Are they, Blahyd? I often wonder whether you seek to build up your faction within *our* faction."

"Tuabir will not turn down a chance to score a great victory and win great booty," said Blade, to turn the conversation away from this touchy area. "And if he values my friendship, he will follow those I follow."

"He will if he values his life," said Cayla shortly. "So be it. That will give us nearly three hundred good fighters. If we cannot make the Count of Tram howl with those, I shall give up my place as a Captain to someone who can!" Blade devoutly wished that last sentence might prove more than a mere verbal flourish.

Recruiting *Thunderbolt* caused more delay. This annoyed Cayla, since there were only about six weeks left for raiding voyages before the winter storms set in. It relieved Blade, however, since he had no desire to see Cayla get any more wealth and influence than she had now, even if his own would increase along with hers. It also gave him more time to consider how best to make his escape from Neral and somehow contrive to make his way to the shores of Royth with Alixa and Brora. He could not conceivably make his own escape and leave them on Neral to face a certain and horrible death.

There could be no way off the southern end of the island. Over the cliffs there was no possible route, unless one were a combination of bird and fish. And there was no way out through the passage. All of those fortifications could keep someone in as easily as keep them out.

Off the northern part of the island, beyond the Mountain? More possible. That area was flat and comparatively unguarded. There were apparently only enough sentries there to keep out casual trespassers and keep in the household and plantation slaves. Some of the wealthier Captains had small villas on the northern slopes of the Mountain and small yachts in creekmouth along the northern coast. If the three of them could make it across the Mountain and manage to steal one of those yachts, and if they could then get a good head start toward the coast of Royth before the alarm was raised—well, the Ocean was large. Even Cayla's influence would hardly be enough to turn out the whole Brotherhood after him. It was a hair-raisingly risky project, but apparently the best hope he had. And in any case, there was no need to do anything serious about it for some months yet, until the end of the coming

67

winter. Trying to sail a small yacht all the way to Royth against the winter storms would simply be a complicated way to commit suicide. Blade firmly put the matter of escape from Neral out of his mind and concentrated on the raid against Tram.

Tuabir had been dubious about the raid at first, but once he had agreed to join it, he drove his own men and the dockyard crews as though sea monsters would swallow them all up if *Thunderbolt* were not ready for sea in three days at the latest. So did Captain Esdros. But enough days still passed to make Cayla short-tempered and snappish before all three ships were manned, equipped, stored, and ready for sea.

Tuabir and Esdros were new as Captains, and Cayla was not one of the most popular ones, so there were no crowds to see them off. Perhaps there would have been none in any case, for they slipped out through the passage in the pale gray light of early dawn, with lanterns still burning to illuminate the dark passage and make the faint curls of foam from the oars glimmer. Clear of the reefs, they raised sail to the brisk following wind and swung away on a broad reach toward the west and their goal.

They sighted the high peak called the Helmet that marked the northeastern corner of Tram only thirteen days out from Neral. Tuabir's navigation had brought the squadron directly to their intended landfall. Almost too close, in fact, since Cayla said there were watchposts on the Helmet that scanned the sea for the approach of hostile fleets. The squadron turned north for half a day, then east again, and it was not until the sun was going down on the fifteenth day of their voyage that Cayla ordered course changed to the south again. She brought out a brass tube, uncapped it, and pulled out a chart yellow with age and frayed with much handling. Blade could recognize the outlines of the land masses, but could not read a single word or number.

Cayla did not bother to explain, but went forward with the chart and a small silver box. She gave strict orders that none were to go forward of amidships until she gave the word. Blade and Brora sat down on the deck, with the

68

rest of the crew behind them. They waited nervously while *Sea Witch* drifted aimlessly and the other two ships formed in a line behind her.

A low murmur from forward made Blade's flesh crawl. Cayla was chanting an incantation. A pungent whiff of the same smoke he had smelled in the underground shrine drifted aft. Then he started violently, feeling his hair stand on end.

Something large was moving in the water just below the bow—something large and living. Blade heard a splashing, the sound of a rough surface dragging across metal, then a prolonged and unmistakable *hissing* noise. Cayla's voice rose again, louder this time, with a note of impatience. The hissing came again. Cayla spoke a single word. Then a quick rasp, a loud splash followed by several smaller ones, and silence.

That silence was broken by a shout from Cayla. "Man the oars, you dogs! Blahyd, you pass my orders on to the steersman. Tell Esdros and Tuabir to follow us exactly, to the stroke." Again, there was a faint splashing sound from ahead, quickly drowned out by the thuds and bangs of the men running to the oars. Slowly *Sea Witch* gathered speed, with Blade standing amidships and relaying Cayla's orders. Brora stood on the stern and watched to see that the other two ships were following them. What they themselves were following, what Cayla had conjured out of the sea, Blade did not care to speculate.

The night was dark, but even in the darkness Blade soon caught the loom of land off to starboard. They were cutting dangerously close to the eastern coast of Tram, through waters the chart showed to be crisscrossed with an impenetrable and lethal maze of reefs. He supposed he should be glad that Cayla had somehow conjured their invisible guide out of the dark sea to lead them, but found he could not manage it.

How long they crept through the darkness behind the thing that swam ahead of them Blade never knew precisely. It was still deep darkness when Cayla suddenly shouted, "Back oars! Let go the anchors!" Blade heard the oar thumps and the rattle and scrape of the anchor chain echoing around them. There was land, high and close by, but invisible in the darkness. He saw the ghostly shapes of *Thunderbolt* and *Spider Prince* range up alongside them, then faint flurries of white as their anchors in turn went down. In the silence that followed, Cayla's voice rose again in a mighty shout of triumph that had no words in it, and was answered by a prolonged hiss from the water and a final tumult of splashing. Blade risked stepping over to the railing just in time to see a faintly glistening mound of water passing aft just beyond the tips of the oars. But what swam beneath that mound and raised it by its passage was still as invisible as it had been all during the night.

Cayla came aft, and for once she came into Blade's arms to be supported and held, as though the night had been too much of a strain even for her iron body and spirit. "I did not think they would answer, after all these years. But they live. They *live*." No need to ask what "they" were.

"Where are we?"

"A small river mouth less than two hours due west of our goal. We will spend the day here, resting, then move against Tram tonight."

"Won't they find us easily here?"

"Here?" She laughed savagely. "Once a temple of our Cult stood here. You will see the ruins when daylight comes. The count who made it ruins laid his curse on the spot and forbade all his subjects to ever pass by. The people's own superstitions will keep them away and us safe."

Gradually the ships settled down for their rest, and gradually also the blackness around them turned gray. In that gray light Blade saw that the three ships were nestled between two steep bluffs, heavily wooded almost down to the water's edge. On top of the bluff to the right, a gaunt tower with windows gaping like the eyes of a skull rose above the trees. Dead black except where vines had struggled up from below, it seemed to brood over past evils— or contemplate future ones. Remembering what inhabited the still, black waters below it, Blade did not wonder that the land around the tower was shunned as cursed. With nothing else to do, he wrapped himself in his cloak and lay down on the deck in the shade of one of the rower's benches. He could not, after this night, bring himself to go below and share Cayla's bed.

CHAPTER 10

Except for six guards on watch aboard each ship, all of the three hundred-odd men in Cayla's squadron slept through most of the day. Toward evening they began to wake and make final preparations—oiling weapons and armor, donning clean clothes, smearing their faces with soot for concealment in the darkness. The armsmasters set up their grinding wheels on deck and put razor edges on any weapon offered to them; the surgeons arrayed their salves and bandages and the less reassuring saws and hammers. By the time it was fully dark, the squadron was ready for action, and Cayla ordered Tuabir and Esdros and their first mates over to *Sea Witch* for a final council of war.

"We will pull alongside the breakwater to the canal and put the landing parties ashore. *Thunderbolt's* men will head straight into town; *Prince's* will move on the harbor. *Witch's* will hold the breakwater and enter the fort where the toll money is stored.

"Remember," she went on, "don't get caught in any serious fighting with regular troops. The local citizenry may be armed, but your men can certainly take care of any shopkeeper rushing out with a club to defend his wares. And don't try to bring any ships away from the harbor. We will have to head north as fast as we can afterwards, and prizes will slow us down. Snatch as much as you can, then set the ships on fire. Do the same thing with the shops in town."

Tuabir looked shocked. Wanton destruction of ships and property was not a pirate habit. They tended to leave what they could not carry away in the hope of being able

71

to some day pay a return visit. But he had sense enough not to protest in those terms. Instead, he said, "If we set the whole cursed town alight, Sister Captain, how are we going to get out of it safely?"

Cayla shrugged. "Use your own judgment. But I want to see a good blaze against the sky before we shove off." Blade had hardly expected her to admit her real reasons for wishing a thorough vengeance on the Counts of Tram.

The sea outside the inlet was almost as calm as that inside. The ships seemed to creep wraithlike across the glassy water. Blade finished his inspection of the crew manning the catapult erected on *Witch's* bow and came back to stand beside Cayla on the quarterdeck. She was grinning savagely, teeth gleaming in her blackened face.

"There will be screams and death tonight in Tram, as there were screams and death in our shrines. Yessssss," trailing off into what seemed to Blade's tense ears horribly like a serpent's hiss. Then she also was silent as the ships continued their slow progress toward Tramport.

Only a little more than the promised two hours later, they saw a yellow light gleaming dimly ahead and beyond it in the darkness a spangle of fainter lights in various colors. "That's the lighthouse on the end of the breakwater," said Cayla. "Alert the catapult crew." Blade went forward and watched as the men wound up their machine and loaded it with a whole cluster of heavy-headed lead bolts. Now the breakwater was clearly visible, silver gray in the darkness, snaking its way out from shore—did *everything* make him think of snakes?—toward the approaching ships.

Suddenly the silence was broken by a shout from ahead. The words came shrill and clear over the water. "Neralers! Neralers! Turn out the guard!" Blade nodded, the catapult twanged, its load of bolts hurtled towards the lighthouse. The light promptly went out. The oarsmen shouted warcries and bent to their oars, sending *Witch* surging ahead.

They crashed alongside the breakwater, and Blade was the first man to leap ashore from the still-moving ship. Men were already swarming toward him from both directions. For a moment he had to whirl and leap like a dervish to keep from being spitted like a fowl. Then more of *Witch*'s men were dropping their oars and scrambling ashore, and the other two ships came sliding in and began disgorging their fighting men too. Blade heard Tuabir's voice bellowing farther up the breakwater. "Move, you sea turtles! We've got a long way to run!" and the clatter of weapons and pounding of feet as his men moved out, brushing through the scattered guards.

The lighthouse was clear of defenders now. Blade stationed half a dozen men with bows to hold it, then led the rest of *Witch*'s landing party up the breakwater behind the other crews. There were already at least a score of bodies littering the breakwater or bobbing in the water beside it. He didn't have time to count whether they were pirates or defenders.

The map showed the toll fort as lying off to the right of the breakwater, up a short path and through a grove of tall trees. He led his men up the path at a trot without incident, but as they reached the trees crossbows suddenly began to twang from inside the grove. Blade saw two of the men behind him topple to the path and lie there writhing. But the whole force of fifty odd pirates were moving so fast that they were closed with their opponents before another volley hurtled from the slow-firing crossbows. Screams, oaths, the clang of swords on swords and the *chunk* of swords carving human flesh rose into the night.

Blade found himself confronted by a grotesquely short man with a plate cuirass, wielding a sword taller than himself with both fury and skill. He steadily gave way before the flailing dwarf, waited until the man was forced by the trees to shorten his stroke, then lunged past his guard into his face. Leaping over the body, Blade reformed his men with bellowed oaths and brandishings of his sword and led them quickly up to the fortress wall.

As a "fort" the toll establishment would never have stood against a major force equipped with even a few siege engines. But Blade's force was one of pirates equipped with nothing but their personal weapons. They would have been baffled utterly by the fort's ditch and

73

single eight-foot wall if Blade had not noticed that several large trees had been allowed to grow within their own height of the wall.

He gave his orders quickly. Archers climbed some of the trees to pick off anyone on top of the wall. Axe men attacked four of the trees nearest to the wall. The remaining pirates drew back under cover. Bows began to twang and axes to flash and hack. "Make those chips fly!" called Blade. "We haven't got all night!"

He had barely finished speaking when with a crackle of splitting wood and breaking branches one of the trees tipped drunkenly, seemed to hang against the sky for a moment, then toppled over with a crash. It slammed straight down onto the wall, making a bridge over both ditch and wall. Blade ran monkeylike up the fallen trunk before it had stopped rocking, sword out and yelling to his men to follow.

Two of the men atop the wall had been crushed into red pulp by the falling tree, but some of their fellows were still alive and fighting. Two of them came at Blade with pikes leveled. He twisted, parried one pike thrust with his sword, grabbed the man by the collar, and slung him bodily off the wall into the ditch. The other drew back, but not fast enough, as Blade's sword whistled down and slashed through the pike shaft and one of the arms holding it. Then others of *Witch's* crew were coming up behind Blade to help clear the wall, and he was able to seize a branch and swing himself down to ground level inside the fort.

Another tree came crashing down and more broken branches and stones pattered down about Blade. He looked around him. Inside the wall was a small flagstoned courtyard, with three buildings set in a rough triangle in the middle of it. As he ran toward the first one, four more soldiers ran out of it. Blade stepped back before their rush, noting almost with detachment their shoddy swordsmanship. This *was* a sleepy and over-confident garrison. In a moment half a dozen of his own men again caught up with him, and the four soldiers died where they stood.

That was very much the story of the whole battle for

74

the fort. Little knots of resistance popped up unexpectedly and chaotically and died minutes later. Perhaps the pirates were clumsy on land, but they were also numerous this night. Not that the pirates escaped unscathed. Six of them were lying dead or dying by the end of the fighting, and more were wounded. But even the dying raised a cheer when Blade, using the keys snatched from the body of the fort's commander, opened the huge iron-shod doors of the vault. Soon they saw their fellows bringing out chest after chest of gold and silver pieces, jewels, fine silks, painted vases, ornamented weapons—everything the Counts of Tram had taken as tolls from passing ships during the months gone past.

It took nearly half Blade's force to simply carry the chests, so he was just as glad there was only one prisoner to guard. The fort commander's daughter was a girl of nineteen, small, blonde, vaguely pretty. She must have been shy and nervous at the best of times and was now fortunately scared almost senseless and certainly far beyond making any attempt to escape. Blade had her hands tied behind her back and one of the pirates led her with a rope around her neck.

The fort's buildings were stone, but everything inside them was blazing as merrily as possible when Blade led his richly encumbered raiders back toward the waiting ships. In the confusion of his own battle, he had almost forgotten about the other two parties. But now as he looked up at the sky, he saw it flaring red and orange over both the town and the harbor. Then as he led his men out of the grove and down the path toward the water, he stopped abruptly.

A solid mass of helmeted and armored men, the heads of their pikes and halberds gleaming in the firelight, had blocked off the end of the breakwater. Blade saw swords and cutlasses flashing just in front of the soldiers, as the pirates tried to break up that solid front, but the wall of points and blades was too strong. Somebody had called out the regular infantry. From what Blade remembered of the Swiss pikemen whom these men resembled, if they once got a good start down that breakwater, they would

75

sweep the pirates aside as inexorably as an advancing tidal wave and then turn to the ships.

Blade was not going to let the pirates become involved in a general disaster like that, regardless of what he might think of them in general, and particularly when Brora—and yes, Tuabir—would be involved in it as well as himself. He quickly gave his orders. Eight of the ablebodied men would stay behind and guard the chests and wounded. The rest—again he waved his sword, this time towards the rear of the infantry formation, and ran down the slope.

As he ran, he noticed a small figure slipping into the water and a bright blonde head swimming up the breakwater until it was just behind the front rank of the infantry. Cayla! Before Blade could wonder what she was doing, he saw her reach up and jerk one infantryman by the ankle. He went over with a yell and a splash. Before the weight of his armor could take him down, she thrust her sword up into the groin of a second man. As he screamed and crumpled, she leaped like a salmon out of the water into the midst of the close-packed soldiers. A moment later, the same mass of soldiers cut off his view of her, and he had too many other things to think about.

Blade's forty men were outnumbered at least five to one by the soldiers, but the soldiers were packed close together and concentrating completely on the enemy to their front. The pirates hit them from behind, by surprise, and at a dead run, yelling like a horde of fiends and laying about them like madmen. Some of the soldiers tried to turn and bring their pikes and halberds to bear. The pirates spitted most of these before they could strike a blow. Some dropped their pole weapons and drew short swords. These lasted a little longer. Some simply dropped everything including helms and armor and ran for it or leaped into the water and swam for it. These mostly got away, because Blade and his men were too busy with the ones who stayed to fight.

Blade was keyed up to the highest pitch, and he was a terrifying sight as he lunged and slashed and hacked and yelled. Run his dagger through the hand of a man trying

76

to bring a halberd down on him, then take the man's head off with a backswing. A swordsman coming at you? Kick him in the knee and then stab him in the neck as he goes over. Blade's sword stuck in the wood of a halberd shaft and was wrenched out of his hands. He let it go, grappled with the halberdier and snapped his neck like a carrot, then darted under a sword thrust and butted the swordsman in the belly so hard that he crashed backward against two of his fellows and all three of them went over the edge of the breakwater to be carried under by the weight of their armor.

There were shouts and yells and running feet behind him, such an uproar that it penetrated even his battle-fogged brain. He turned to see Tuabir, carrying off all things a quarterstaff, charging toward the breakwater at the head of his crew. They too were yelling like fiends. Blade saw the soldiers turn toward the new attack. Then by one accord and at one instant they broke, and there was a mad scramble to shuck off armor, helms, and weapons and get into the water and safety.

Not all of them found it. The archers in the lighthouse had plenty of light and great sport. And Blade saw Cayla splashing merrily about in the water, as at home as any seal or otter, coming up behind soldiers, jerking their heads back, and smoothly cutting their throats. The water was blotched with red patches when she finally pulled herself out of the water and came up to Blade.

Her shirt was hanging in shreds about her waist, and there was a feather-thin red line across the skin of her left breast. All of the rest of the blood that dyed her trousers was from her score or more victims. She was maddening and deadly and frightening and beautiful, and Blade felt nothing strange for once in reaching out and pulling her against him.

A cough from Tuabir interrupted him. "Sister Captain, Master Blahyd. I see Esdros' men coming up across the canal bridge. I judge it were time we were thinking of gathering ourselves together and making for the open sea."

"True," said Cayla slowly, as if reluctant to leave before she had thought up some other way of wreaking vengeance on the Counts of Tram. "A good night's work we've had."

"The night isn't over," said Tuabir with a note of impatience in his voice. "And we'd best be putting what's left of it to use in getting well clear of here before the war fleet comes down on us."

Cayla nodded sharply, and all her dreaminess left her. She began barking orders with all her normal briskness, and soon men and booty were streaming aboard all three ships. Without waiting to stow or count the booty, the men took their places at the oars, the lines were cast off, and the last sentries recalled. All three ships backed hastily out into the approaches of the canal, turned north, and fled away as fast as their battle-weary rowers could thrust them along.

Half the sky was filled with a bloody glow behind them as they pounded along. Cayla, a blanket hastily wrapped around her, stood watching it as it slowly receded behind them. Blade went up to her and said, "Captain, how do we break through to the open sea?" He swallowed. "Do we use the same—method—we used coming in?"

Cayla turned at the note in his voice and glared at him. "You dislike the Guardians of the Cult?" Blade had sense enough to shake his head. "No, Blahyd, we head straight north. Before long we will come to the coast of a wide stretch of land long in dispute between Mardha and the neighboring barbarians to the north. It is a wild land, shunned by most. But there are numbers of little creeks and river mouths. We can find fresh water and lie concealed until the count's warfleet has exhausted its rowers beating up and down in search of us. And we can divide the booty and perhaps find some entertainment." There was a glint in her eyes as she said that last word that made Blade feel vaguely uneasy.

CHAPTER 11

A series of rainsqualls lasting through most of the morning helped them break through the first line of patrols. The only ship challenged was *Thunderbolt*, but with her masts down and most of her crew below at the oars she looked enough like a local warship to pass by safely. This incident again confirmed Blade's low opinion of the efficiency of the count's armed forces. He began to wonder if it might not be possible to organize a pirate fleet large enough to occupy the whole County for several weeks and carry away everything that wasn't nailed down. Then he realized that he was thinking perhaps too much like a pirate of Neral. As usual, he was slipping deep into the pattern of thoughts of what he was supposed to be and retaining only a tenuous connection with the Richard Blade of Home Dimension.

Some thirty hours from Tramport, just before dawn, *Sea Witch* led her squadron into an almost landlocked bay. Not content with that, Cayla had the three ships pull almost to the rear of the bay into the mouth of a small river flowing into it. She ordered the exhausted and staggering crews ashore to cut branches and bushes to tie all over the ships, then personally supervised the backbreaking job of dismounting two of the catapults and remounting them under cover to guard the entrance to the bay. This work took most of the day, and only occasional rain showers that drenched their sweating bodies kept most of the crewmen from collapsing in their tracks. Finally, when Cayla was satisfied that all that could be done had been done, she gave the order for sleep. Most of the men dropped where they stood and slept like the dead on the bare planks for twelve hours, oblivious to further showers. Blade unashamedly did the same. Twenty men with clubs could have taken the whole squadron and everybody in it, but they were not bothered.

Still, it was two full days more before Cayla decided they could let down their guard enough to do what everybody had been waiting for since they left the burning town—divide the booty. That, as Blade had heard, could be a bloody mess under a weak captain. But none of the captains or mates here were weak, so the division went smoothly.

There was much to divide. About two hundred thousand Roythan crowns—no record for the pirates, but enough to make the captains and officers wealthy men and keep even the boys who aided the cooks and carpenters in comfort for several years. There was a large amount in silver and gold coins and almost an equal amount in jewels, worked gold, and silver ornaments. There were enough fancy weapons to arm the whole crew of the squadron twice over, several hundred bolts of silk and other valuable fabrics, and assorted boxes of spices and drugs, including a box of the blue dream powder which Cayla promptly threw overboard.

When Cayla was through supervising the division, and then through gloating, she turned to the prisoners. Although Blade's party had brought back only the one girl, the others had been more fortunate and had scooped up half a dozen influential citizens (or citizens who had looked influential) in the town itself and three ship captains and an army officer too drunk to fight in the harbor area. These promised a tidy sum in ransoms.

Cayla took even more complete charge of dealing with the prisoners than she had of dividing the other spoils. Tuabir and Esdros stood well behind her. Blade suspected that in Tuabir's case at least it was because he had no wish to be associated with Cayla's methods of treating the prisoners.

As each was brought before her, she barked a command, "Kneel!" Those who were a split second slow in going down on their knees had her light but deadly whip laid aross their faces and would go down with blood dripping into the sand. Then she would stride up and down in front of them, snapping out questions. Name? Order? Family? Fortune? Skills, if any? And so on. Sometimes she would stop in front of the captive with a sinuous swaying of her body that reminded Blade of a snake swaying in front of a bird it wanted to charm. If the captive looked up—and most men did—*crack* would go the whip again, and more blood would be dripping into the sand.

Most of the prisoners, once properly humiliated, were admitted to ransom. Some of them, Blade suspected, would never be free again, seeing the way they blanched and groaned when the ransom figures were read out. The captive officer, however, was kept kneeling for a particularly long time. Finally, Cayla turned to Blade and said, "What say you, Blahyd? Do you think anyone will consider a soldier—an officer—who was too drunk to fight worth ransoming?"

Considering what usually happened to officers caught drunk on duty in Home Dimension, Blade had to shake his head. "Well, then," said Cayla, "I think we will make a slave of this one. He should be good for a year or two on the farms at least. His limbs are thick, even thicker than his head."

The man howled wordlessly and threw himself face down in the sand. Then, as Cayla stepped over toward him with the whip ready, he suddenly sprang up and lunged at her. One huge hand was already clutching at the hilt of her dagger when one of the guards whipped up his pike and hurled it like a spear straight at the officer's back. It caught him just below the shoulder blades and drove clear through him and out his chest, narrowly missing Cayla's leg as it did so. She jumped back as the man toppled forward and lay without a twitch.

"Good eyes and a good hand, there, sailor," she said to the guard. "Two extra gold pieces for you from my personal share." Two gold pieces, Blade knew, were enough to satisfy most of a sailor's wants for the better part of a year. He was not surprised when the guard gaped and grinned and stammered his thanks.

Now the guards brought the last prisoner forward—the fort commander's daughter, the only woman among the prisoners. Cayla's expression as she watched the girl made

Blade uneasy, and the silky note in her voice as she spoke made him swallow and wait for whatever was coming in a cold sweat.

He did not have long to wait. The girl's name was Dynera, and now that her father was dead, she had no family left. None? No one who might pay a ransom?.

"Please—I—I—no. My mother—she was descended from Count Prasin the Fourth. But she was an orphan. All I had was my f-f-father," and she burst into tears.

Blade saw Cayla's eyes flare at the mention of the Count and shuddered. Prasin the Fourth had been the greatest of all the persecutors of the Cult. The poor girl had just signed her own death warrant, and now the snake would strike.

"Prasin the Fourth? Indeed, child, you come from a high lineage! The present count—you are sure he will not consider a ransom, for your mother's sake if not your own?"

"N-n-no. My mother's parents were—were out of favor at c-c-court, and—"

"Then I say you *lie*! And I will prove it on your body!" *Whap-crack* the whip slashed across the girl's face. She screamed and clapped her hands to her cheeks. Cayla stepped close until she loomed over the girl and glared down at her. "By the Law of the Woman's Duel, you can prove that you are what you say by besting me in equal combat. We will even release you without ransom." At those words, the girl looked up, with the beginnings of hope in her eyes. "Yes, freedom! Would you rather fight for it, or shall I have you spread-eagled here on the sand and turned over to my crew before you die?" The girl blanched and murmured:

"I will fight."

"Good!" There was an unholy lust in that one word. "Your weapons?"

The girl looked around her, the expression in her eyes reminding Blade even more than before of a trapped bird. "I—I'll take a sword." Blade had to close his eyes for a moment to fight off the nausea. The girl had probably never handled any weapon more lethal than a fruit knife in her life. Yet here she was taking up a sword to fight one of the deadliest women Blade had ever seen. She would have no chance—no chance to do anything except provide a few minutes' obscene pleasure for Cayla and the more loutish among the pirates.

Cayla did not put off her pleasure. One of the pirates threw the girl a sword and she picked it up and waved it a couple of times. Blade saw that she was quite as inexperienced as he had suspected. But then he remembered that sometimes the rank amateur, by doing the unexpected, can defeat the professional who is trained only in dealing with other professionals. Blade of course had no hope that with Cayla dead the girl would be released. Her death would still be slow and agonizing. But with Cayla dead, at least all her monstrous plans would fall with her, and his own situation would be much simpler.

Cayla did nothing to prepare herself for the fight beyond kicking off her boots and knotting a sweat band around her head. Then she stepped forward into the thirty-foot square of sand marked out with ropes strung from oars. From her side, the girl stepped forward, the sword held out in front of her as though it were a snake that might turn and bite her.

"Be you ready?" Cayla called out, in the formal Duel query.

The girl stammered, "R-ready."

Cayla raised her weapons—the whip and the foot-long, razor-edged dagger. But she did not dart forward. Blade knew that if she had done so, she could have had the girl dead on the sand in a matter of seconds. She was going to play with the poor creature. His stomach churned, but he kept it under control by a great effort.

Now the girl rushed in, the sword swinging wide and whistling around. She had strong wrists, at least. But Cayla was cat-quick, ducking the wild stroke and coming up, not with the dagger but with the whip full force across the girl's stomach. She gasped and jumped back.

Now Cayla came in, the dagger flashing up and out in a stroke deliberately timed to whistle past the girl's cheek and rip her ear. Blood trickled again. Cayla danced aside

83

from the girl's wild return slash, darted in again, and this time the dagger slashed the shoulder of the girl's blouse open without touching the skin below. The girl blushed as the blouse drooped down, half-baring one breast, but made no effort to strip the rest of the blouse off. Instead, she rushed Cayla again, the sword fanning the air in front of her. The pirate woman used neither dagger nor whip this time. She dropped backward onto her hands and kicked out with both feet as the girl came within range. Both feet slammed into Dynera's stomach and the girl gasped explosively and sat down with a thump. Before she could rise, Cayla was up again, pinning her sword arm to the ground with one foot. Cayla reached down and laid the whip across the hand holding the sword. It opened and the sword lay on the sand. Cayla kicked it away without taking her eyes off the girl.

After that, Blade's memory stopped recording the details of the fight. All he remembered afterwards was that it went on and on and on, with far too many of the pirates cheering wildly. It went on until the girl lay in the sand naked, bloody, dead.

Cayla stood up, threw her dagger and whip down on the bloody sand, and came toward Blade. "Well fought," he managed to croak. He could not have reached out to her or touched her to become King of Royth. He barely managed to avoid vomiting until he had made his way some fifty paces into the forest and was out of sight of the beach and the people on it.

He was completely empty, not only internally but emotionally, when he got to his feet and became conscious of somebody standing behind him. His sword was out and he was whirling around to strike before he recognized Tuabir.

"Well, Master Blahyd. Our lady fiend has had her fun for this trip. Your own lady is safe for the moment."

"My lady?"

"Aye, the Lady Alixa. If you're watchful of Cayla when she casts an eye on Alixa, you'll see what'll give you no pleasure. And one of these days you may well see her challenging your lady to use her the way she used that poor girl today."

The idea would have made Blade sick again, if there had been anything left inside him. As it was, he only shook his head helplessly.

"Ah well, it'll be some time before Cayla wants her fun again. Maybe between now and then you can think of something to do about it."

CHAPTER 12

The obvious thing to do about Cayla was to kill her. Blade thought about that all during the four weeks it took the squadron to beat its way back to Neral. It was a tedious and grueling trip, the last week spent fighting against almost continuous westerly gales which several times blew them out of sight of the island. When the squadron finally landed, too sea-tossed and weary to properly appreciate the welcome laid on for them, Blade was no nearer a solution than he had been the night the squadron sailed from its refuge.

The problems were mostly caused by Cayla's own sharp wits. She had noticed more of Blade's reaction to the duel than he would have had her notice. The night afterwards she calmly informed him that of course he could kill her any time he wished, and perhaps he would get away with it. She was not so popular among the Captains that they would really exert themselves to catch her murderer, particularly if the circumstances were uncertain. But she did have a respectable number of friends and allies, and these would ensure that Alixa and Brora both died soon and unpleasantly, whatever happened to her. And she might challenge Alixa and put her down in a way that would make Dynera's death look pleasurable by comparison, if she judged Blade was plotting against her.

If Blade had only had himself to worry about, he would probably have run Cayla through on the spot and taken his chances. But he could not and would not throw away his companions' lives along with his own, so he held his hand and his peace. But he made no pretense of being able to share Cayla's bed after the duel. He would much rather have slept in a nest of cobras.

When they finally reached Neral the situation worsened. Perhaps Cayla had not been popular before, but now that she had conceived and carried out the most daring and profitable raid the Brotherhood had to its credit for the past three years, her stock soared. So did Blade's, fortunately. He had, after all, fought heroically and led the counterattack on the Tramian infantry that had saved the whole expedition. But the lion's share of the glory was Cayla's, and Blade saw far too many of those who had previously avoided her begin to cluster around what they saw to be a rising star in the Brotherhood. She was now much closer to being unassailable.

Blade had ample leisure to contemplate this fact, because winter gales were closing the seas to honest commerce and pirate raiding alike. It had been more than two generations since the half-legendary Dystronos of Cral led five ships across the winter seas in the teeth of wind and snow to plunder shipping in the very High Port of Royth itself. On the occasional calm and clear day, ships would indeed make their way out through the passage to exercise their men at the oars and help them keep their sea legs, but none went out of sight of Neral. Even with this precaution, two galleys attempting a night passage of the reefs to avoid being caught at sea by a gale took the ground and were pounded to pieces, drowning better than a hundred and fifty men.

Many of the pirates spent their winters in debauchery, spending whatever gains they had made during the season of raiding and inevitably ending up the next spring penniless, if not in fact many silver bits in debt to the brothels and shopkeepers. Blade, however, spent his enforced leisure maintaining his proficiency in arms, memorizing charts and sailing instructions for all parts of the Ocean, and, very rarely, roaming about the northern end of the island. He had to face the fact that the only way to safety for him and his companions lay in escaping from Neral entirely. By the time spring came, he meant to be ready.

And it was important for more than the three of them to make their escape in spring. All the evidence he had gathered and put down in a secret set of ciphered notes told him that Indhios' plots were going to come to fruition next spring or summer as well, and he had to reach Royth and carry the warning, somehow.

Seeing that sharing her bed revolted him, and recognizing that sex had never given her much influence over him in any case, Cayla consented to his taking quarters of his own. He was not yet ranked as a Captain (although she planned to have him promoted in time for the spring voyages), so Blade took a three-room apartment in one of the more expensive boarding houses on the terrace below. Cayla visited him occasionally to take a cup of hot wine and enlarge on her plans for the future.

At other times, Alixa came to him. It had come hard for this sensual young noblewoman to sleep alone when Cayla had dragged Blade off for her own purposes and pleasures. Now, wasting no further time in jealousy after her initial flare of rage, she returned to him, visiting his quarters as often as she could find Brora, Tuabir or some trustworthy sailor chosen by them to escort her through the dark streets of the pirate city. She never stayed more than an hour or two, for Blade was by no means certain that Cayla was not in fact giving both him and Alixa enough rope to hang themselves. Their lovemaking was intense and sometimes exultant, but always crammed into too short a time for either of them. Gradually, Blade came to wonder whether Cayla had in fact abandoned her claims to him as her Companion.

Then came a night in the dead of winter. "Dead" indeed—as Blade stood at the window and stared out into the darkness, it seemed that the whole world was in fact dead. No moon, no stars, no wind or snow, nothing moving below in the street. Only a single yellow puddle of light from a lamp hanging from someone's front door. It would be easy for Alixa to reach the house, and once she was there they would finally have the whole night ahead of them. Blade was much too lusty a man to tolerate having his pleasures in rationed installments.

He was so busy anticipating his pleasures that he almost ignored the knock on the door. Even then, he had to move down the stairs cat-footed to avoid waking the other mates and factors and shopkeepers who shared the house. Opening the door, he saw Alixa's face grinning into his from her blue hood, and behind her Brora, his face strained, his eyes roving watchfully, frost on his brown beard and hair. He took Alixa's outstretched hand and led her up the stairs, Brora following at a discreet distance, his hand never far from the hilt of his cutlass.

She was urgent and tumultuous in her love-making that night, more than ever before, gasping and crying out with each climax, and so stimulating Blade every time she felt him flagging that he reached new heights of his own. In time, it was sheer exhaustion that led them to collapse, limp and sweat-glazed, amid the tangled sheets.

Sleep was just beginning to drift over Blade when he heard a rattle and a bang from above. Somebody or something was climbing down through the roof hatch. He reached out of bed to pluck his sword from the floor and his dagger from its boot sheath, but did not light the lantern, murmuring to Alixa, "Don't move."

Feet sounded on the attic stair. He heard Brora draw his sword and step in front of the door; then the attic door burst open with a crash. A moment later the door into his own rooms flew inward off its hinges. Before it had hit the floor, Blade had rolled out of the bed on the far side, so that he was invisible from the doorway.

Cayla charged into the room with a cutlass flashing in one hand and her whip cracking in the other. "Whore!" she shouted, with a note of indignation in her voice that sounded grotesquely false to Blade. "Bed with my Companion, will you? Accept my Challenge, or die here in your foul bed!" Alixa played her part well, moaning and shivering wordlessly as she clasped the bedclothes about her. Cayla darted across the room, raising her whip, and as she did so Blade sprang to his feet and slashed at her in a deadly overhand stroke that should have split her like a salted fish.

Instead, his feet tangled in the fallen blankets as he

rose, throwing him off balance, and the sword whistled harmlessly down past Cayla and hit the floor with a tremendous clang. Cayla sprang back, and Esdros, with more courage than craft, charged in. Blade had only to raise the sword point and let the young Captain spit himself on it. He went down with a gurgle and a scream. Blade jerked his sword free and turned to face Cayla.

But that lady saw no place in her plans for a fair duel against Blade. She backed out of the door at almost the same furious pace at which she had entered, Blade hard after her. As he charged through the door the two bravos who had Brora trapped in an angle of the corridor turned to face him, not fast enough to do themselves much good but fast enough for their mistress to vanish down the main stairs. Blade's massive fist smashed into the face of the first bravo, hurling him backward onto the other's sword. Both went down, and before either could rise Brora had thrust twice, and both stayed down.

"Master Blahyd," said the sailor, "I think we were best thinkin' to take our leave." Blade nodded.

"Brora, go and barricade the stairs to keep anyone from coming up until we're ready to leave." He darted into the bedroom. "Alixa. Put on some warm clothing and get stout shoes and a dagger." She scrambled out of bed and began rummaging through his clothing chests. As tall as she was, she could wear his clothing with little difficulty.

A new uproar of feet and voices sounded on the stairs below as the rest of the tenants woke up and took notice. Blade heard Brora's voice bellowing, "An affair of the Brotherhood! Send for a Captain Councillor!" Sending for one of the Brotherhood's ruling body as a trouble-shooter would effectively keep prying eyes and ears busy for a few more minutes. Blade joined Alixa at the clothing chests and began his own hurried dressing.

They left the house through the same roof hatch that Cayla and her party had used, dropping down to the street level as soon as they had reached the next roof. Once the alarm was given, anybody seen clambering across the rooftops would be a marked man, and they could move faster along the streets anyway. So far there was no sign of alarm—the streets were as dark and silent as before.

Blade gambled on their having at least a few minutes before the hunt began and took the most direct route up the slope to the road that led toward the Mountain. If they passed safely over the Mountain and reached the northern end of the island, they would at least have room to run and dodge.

They passed the sentries at the entrance to the Captains' street without difficulty, walking slowly, like any three sailors returning from a carousal. Blade and Alixa kept their hoods pulled low over their faces, which were better known than Brora's.

A long flight of stone stairs led from the Captains' street up the slope to the rim of the great bowl and the road around its rim. As they climbed higher, the great sullen dark mass of the port and harbor spread out farther and farther below them, faint yellow and red specks marking where a party or dockyard work was going on late.

They were more than two-thirds of the way up the stairs when suddenly half a dozen smoky orange fires began spitting sparks in the darkness below, and twenty furiously beaten gongs began to clamor. It became a greater effort than before to hold to walking pace, but all the more important. They still had to get past the sentries at the top of the stairs, a least, while attracting a minimum of attention.

There were four of the sentries, looking glum, weary, and chilled to the bone. Blade nodded casually to them as he climbed up on the level, but was rewarded by a stiff nod fom the leader.

"Hold, sirs."

"Eh?" Pretend to be drunk, and hope they'll think it too much trouble to start an interrogation.

"The alarm's gone. Nobody gets past here without the word of a Captain."

"Ah—um?"

"Sorry, sirs. Don't know what's happened, probably nothing, but—" breaking off suddenly as Alixa's hood

90

slipped off her face. He wasted a fatal second staring, just long enough for Blade and Brora to whip out sword and cutlass and ram both into his chest. He crumpled, rolled over the top step, and kept on rolling.

Blade and Brora were too busy disposing of the other three to watch his progress down into the darkness. Two they chopped down with little effort; the third defended himself for a moment, then dropped his weapon and ran screaming off into the darkness. By the mercy of Druk—or whoever was watching over them—he ran *away* from the Mountain and its guardposts. If he had run the other way—Blade shuddered at the notion of trying to climb over the bare rock ridges of the Mountain to avoid squads of alerted sentries at the passes.

Now the thing to do was to make as much noise as possible, but try to make it the sort of noise the guards would be expecting. Blade threw his hood back and broke into a run, Brora and Alixa at his heels, all three shouting at the top of their lungs, "Haro, hallo, hi! Guard, guard, turn out the guard!"

It was a good mile and a half, mostly uphill, to the gate at the first pass. All three of them were half-winded by the time they reached it. Blade saw as they approached that the guard had certainly turned out. But they held their pikes and cutlasses casually, hardly imagining that these three figures running plainly up to them and bellowing like bulls could be trying to avoid them.

The guard commander recognized Blade, but merely greeted him.

"What trouble, Master Blahyd?"

"Great trouble! Some villains have slain all four of the guards at the top of the main stairs!"

"Druk be merciful."

"Yes, there's deadly work a-foot tonight. I've been ordered to head through the pass and set up a guard on that side with the sentries from the northern posts."

"Wise." The guard commander paused for a moment, then said, "Would you like to take three of our horscs? We keep them for the quick sending of messages. This seems full as important."

Blade almost laughed out loud at the notion of their getting, literally, a free ride over the pass, then nodded. Two of the horses were already saddled and bridled. Blade ordered Brora and Alixa to mount and be ready to move at his signal, while he himself waited, showing impatience and continuously expecting somebody to come yelling up the road to tell the guard commander the truth.

Two small figures indeed had appeared at the far end of the road by the time the third horse was ready. Blade sailed into the saddle without touching the stirrups and threw the guard captain a gold piece. "For you and your men, for your service to the Brotherhood tonight!"

"Thank you, Master Blahyd. And may Druk be with you tonight!"

As they cantered off toward the pass, Brora turned in his saddle and grinned to Blade as he said, "Druk had better be w'him, Master, when they finds out who he've let through and e'en sped on their way!" Blade nodded, then turned to concentrate on keeping his horse moving along the road.

Although twisting and narrow, the road was well surfaced, and in less than an hour they were eight good miles north of the pass and entering the forest belt. Blade led the others off the road into the forest to let the horses breathe and told them of their situation.

"We're ill-equipped, compared to what I had planned. What's worse, we're going to have to risk the voyage to Royth in the teeth of the winter gales. But we should be able to raid a villa or two for food and clothing, then head for the coast and trust to Druk."

"Aye, trust that he'll make us a miracle! Have ye thought, Master Blahyd, that all the yachts most likely be pulled up out o'·t' sea for the winter? And if we be lucky and get to sea, whyfore make for Royth? W' the winds at our backs, we might reach Mardha in half the time and w' half the danger."

Blade had considered and rejected that very idea. "Because we also have to warn somebody in Royth about what the pirates are planning."

Brora nodded and Alixa nodded too, but also frowned.

"Well and good. But if that is what you plan to do when you reach Royth, remember that you will find Count Indhios almost as deadly an enemy as the pirates."

"We'll worry about that when we land in Royth," said Blade. He had learned that one of the surest roads to disaster in a tough situation was exhausting yourself with premature worrying. "And Indhios at least is only one man, not fifty thousand." He dug his heels into his horse and led his companions back onto the road.

They were not challenged once during the night, by a miracle. In fact, they might have been riding across an island of the dead, except for the lights they saw gleaming in occasional slave huts. Toward morning, and toward the far northern end of the island, they sought out the deepest and gloomiest patch of forest they could find, tethered the horses, rolled themselves up as warmly as possible in their cloaks, and slept for a few hours.

Blade was awakened by the sound of horses passing on the road. Although he knew the hard-frozen ground would retain little or no trace of their own passage, still he gripped his sword and lay motionless, listening until he heard the horses move on. There was no need to tell his companions what that sound meant. The hunt was on. They would have to abandon their own horses and from here on rely on stealth.

If there were any yachts in the water now, they would most likely be on the eastern or leeward side of Neral, sheltered from the westerly gales that could move boulders the size of houses and leave frozen spray on rocks three hundred feet above the water. As soon as it was dark, they moved out, all three muffled to the eyes, Blade and Brora with their hands never far from their weapons.

Twice they had to scuttle hastily for cover as mounted patrols clattered past. Once they nearly blundered into view of the sentries walking a slow beat around a cluster of slave huts almost concealed in a grove. Several times they stumbled over roots or dead branches and fell painfully on the frozen ground. Never did they find a boat that was both in the water and in Brora's opinion sturdy enough to have any hope of carrying them to Royth.

Toward morning it began to snow. Blade realized that they would have to get food before they could resume the search. The long hours in the cold had Alixa worn and pale, and both Blade and Brora were feeling the strain also. But approaching any inhabited place meant risking discovery and proclaiming their presence to the searching patrols. Yet they had no choice. With rumbling bellies they fell to the ground and wrapped themselves up once more for their day's fitful sleep.

Night again. The lights from the windows of the slave huts squatting by the frost-covered beach looked almost cheerful to the three half-frozen figures gliding toward them, their eyes on the storehouse at the end of the row. A bluff to their left hid most of the little bay from Blade's view, but as far as he could see toward the open ocean, it was clear of patrolling ships within easy hail. He drew his sword and motioned the other two to follow him.

He was so intent on moving quietly and thinking so much of the bread and dried fish that filled the storehouse ahead, that he failed to catch the first warning crack of twigs behind him. Then he heard Alixa start to scream, gasp, and squeal in panic as a hand clamped down over her mouth. He spun ground to see two large men in shaggy coats jerking Alixa into the air until her feet kicked frantically. Brora sprawled face down in the nee- dles, his sword lying a foot beyond his outflung hand.

An ambush! Blade whipped his sword up to the guard position and sprang backward, seeking a tree to protect his rear. As he did so more footsteps crackled behind him. Before he could complete another quick turn, something heavy and hard smashed down on his head. He felt his knees giving, but blackness swallowed him up before he could feel his face slamming down on the ground.

CHAPTER 13

When Blade awoke, his first reaction was one of surprise that there was a soft, comfortable bed under him, and not the damp stone floor of a prison cell with perhaps a little moldy straw thrown down on it. Then he looked about him and realized that he was in the Captain's cabin of *Thunderbolt*. From the steady rolling motion under him and the creak of timbers, he knew the ship was at sea. Then the door opened, admitting first a blast of icy wind, then Tuabir. The sailor was grinning broadly.

"The surgeon said you'd be with us soon, so I came by to answer all the questions I knew you'd be asking."

Blade nodded, then decided that wasn't such a good idea. He found enough of his voice to ask, "Are we—prisoners?"

Tuabir looked indignant. "I—haul you back to face Cayla's bravos? The caretaker my lads were helping bag you thinks so, but what he doesn't know won't hurt him—or you." He seemed to take it for granted that no further answer was needed. And for the moment Blade agreed with him. But there were other questions.

"Where are we going?"

"Thunderbolt's following a course due west. We're hoping to make landfall at Cape Xera, Druk willing, in about three weeks' time."

So they were going to Royth after all. But:

"What about you—and the crew? Won't—?"

"All of the crew yet living are with me in this." That remark, Blade felt, left out a few details. "King Pelthros has a name for being easy with pardons to pirates who come to him of their own will, giving up the pirate life and swearing by Druk to be peaceable and honest to the end of their days." Tuabir almost managed to say that with a straight face. Then he sobered and went on.

"I'm not feeling any great joy at giving up the Brotherhood. But now that Cayla has them eating out of her filthy white hand, there'll be no justice for any who go against her. Perhaps you should have stayed and fought her in the Council, for it was your running off that made her story believed as much as anything else. But no matter—you did what you thought was the best. It would have been a chancy thing to speak out anyway." He shrugged.

"Has she revealed some of her—her other plans?"

"For the moment, no. There are many in her camp having no wish to strike a blow for the Serpent Priestesses of Mardha, who'd yet strike mighty blows against the Kingdom of Royth."

"Yes, and she'll rebuild the Serpent shrines on the Kingdom's ruins. We must stop her!" Blade stopped, realizing that the blow on his head must still be addling his wits, to make him say such a foolishly obvious thing.

But Tuabir only grinned and said, "And after me just telling you why fourscore good men are forswearing the Brotherhood to take you to Royth. . . . Ah well, you're needing more sleep, I think."

Blade slept another twelve full hours, and when he awoke after that he was calm, clear-headed, and ravenously hungry. Alixa came in to bring him a tray of food and stayed afterwards for conversation and other things. They lay curled against each other in the bed while *Thunderbolt* beat her way westward, mile by mile.

As he paced the deck and looked out at the heaving gray sea, Tuabir expected that it would be some days before anyone even thought of hunting for them, assuming that he had been driven out to sea by bad weather. And it would be more days yet before they decided whether to send out ships to search, and even then they would probably decide against it. And then he thought of the risks *he* was running for the man who lay below in the Captain's cabin, risks that would keep Captains older and more experienced than he was in port. Most of Tuabir's nearly fifty years had been spent learning other things than philosophy, but he sometimes wondered now whether this Blahyd was not a man sent by Druk to influence many other men's destinies. And when he had finished that thought, he would shrug and grin and go stamping aft, calling for hot wine.

Whether by Druk's favor, Tuabir's and Brora's good seamanship, the stout hull of *Thunderbolt,* or merely common garden-variety luck, they made Tuabir's intended landfall only two days beyond his intended three weeks. Watching Cape Xera loom out above the gray feathers of mist that spread across the gently heaving swells, Blade had a feeling of relief that he quickly reined in. It was a case of "so far, so good."

"Now we need to find ourselves a port," he said. "One where Indhios isn't likely to be in control. And one where the garrison isn't going to be so nervous that they sound the alarm and call out the fleet before we can explain ourselves."

"Srodki is the nearest," put in Tuabir, looking at the chart.

"Aye, and part of the Chancellor's personal holdin' too. We'd be a flea leapin' into a furnace if we went in there," said Brora shortly.

"Then what of Pyreira?" said Tuabir. "It's next beyond Srodki. We'll be in more danger of storms than of men if we go on cruising hither and yon offshore."

"True indeed," replied Brora. "Aye, Pyreira it must be, then. But I little like passin' north about the Ayesh Islands this time o' the year. Be we get a norwester and we've a good chance o' bein' driven straight among 'em."

The northwester that Brora had feared was already beginning to rise by nightfall when they rounded the northern tip of Grand Ayesh. *Thunderbolt* pitched with a steadily fiercer motion that forced Blade to hang on to the railing as he walked back and forth with Tuabir, inspecting the rigging. By midnight, they had to abandon any attempt to use the oars. The rowers could hardly sit on their benches, the oars as often as not flailed uselessly in the air, and the pumps were hard at work to throw out the water that poured in the oar ports every time *Thunderbolt* stuck her nose in deep. If they had been in no haste, they would long since have turned and run before the gale. As it was, it was nearly two in the morning before Tuabir came up to Blade and suggested that course of action.

Blade agreed. For all the small-boat sailing he had done in Home Dimension and his crash course in seamanship here, he was still an amateur where Tuabir and Brora were professionals.

To run before the gale, *Thunderbolt* first had to be turned broadside to the rising sea, an operation even Blade knew to be dangerous. The tiller was triple-manned and the rowers took their places. One side's rowers were ready to push, the others to pull, in order to swing the ship around before the waves could capsize her.

The darkness was now almost total. The wind blew sheets of spray out of a blackness as deep as that of the Pit itself. Only by judging the motion of the ship could Tuabir tell the best moment to turn. Blade saw him standing spraddle-legged as the deck heaved under him. Then he cupped both hands over his mouth and bellowed into the gale, "Coming about!"

Blade felt the motion of the ship change from a pitch to a roll and clung to the railing as the deck tilted over to a fifty-degree angle and green water sluiced over the leeward railing. For a long moment *Thunderbolt* hung there, tilted over at a preposterous angle and lurching slowly around onto her new course. The deck was just beginning to tilt back to something more normal when with a tremendous boom and crash a wave larger than any before roared out of the night. *Thunderbolt* heaved herself up in a wicked corkscrewing motion. From aft Blade heard a tremendous smashing and splintering sound.

As the wave passed away under them and the water poured off the decks, Blade saw Tuabir coming rapidly forward. "The rudder's gone!" he gasped.

Blade had a short moment's we're-doomed feeling, then said, "We'll have to steer with the oars. Thank Druk this is a galley."

"Aye. A sailing ship would be finished here. And if we can't keep off the rocks, we'll be finished too. Druk grant us a beach for a landing place."

98

For the next three hours, there was nothing but the whistle of the wind, the hiss and boom of the waves, the monotonous clanking of the pumps, and the occasional thumpings of the oars. Tuabir and Brora made no effort to keep the men continuously rowing. Only when *Thunderbolt* threatened to swing round again broadside to the waves did Brora bellow orders, in a voice that was beginning to crack with fatigue and strain, to keep the oars moving until the ship was safe again.

Tuabir hoped the gale might drive them far enough east to let them clear the northern tip of Grand Ayesh. Once clear of the land, they could ride out the gale at sea and then when it subsided row back to the first convenient landing place. But when a miserable gray dawn crept tentatively over the sea, the long, dark line of Grand Ayesh's north coast was clearly visible, stretching too far to leave them with any hope of clearing it.

There were nowhere near enough boats for all the men aboard, and even if there had been, no boat could live in the boiling surf that thundered around the approaching rocks. Their only hope was to cling to *Thunderbolt* herself until she took the ground, then swim for it, unless by some miracle they drove ashore on sand, in which case the ship might stay in one piece long enough for the gale to subside.

Except for a handful of men at the oars to keep the ship end to waves that were getting shorter and more jumbled as the water shoaled, the whole crew was up on deck now. Brora was busily making ready a long rope, with which he hoped to swim to shore. At Tuabir's orders, most of the crew discarded seaboots, long coats, and everything else that might weigh them down in the water. Most of them, like Blade, stripped to shirt and trousers, a dagger, and a pouch on their belt. Blade's pouch, apart from a flint-and-steel lighter, held Duke Khystros' signet ring and the notes on the pirate conspiracy, securely wrapped in oiled leather.

The seas were steep and ragged now. The wind blew the spray from their tops in a continuous sheet. The men aboard *Thunderbolt* were as wet as if they had already been in the water. A jagged black slab of rock reared itself out of the water to port, the waves geysering spray in fifty-foot sheets as they beat against it. The water was shoaling fast now. Blade and Tuabir stood in the very bow, trying to pierce the gloom and spray and make out what kind of land lay dead ahead.

Then there was a grinding, a cracking sound, and a tremendous jolt that seemed to slam Blade's spine up through the top of his head. Not a man aboard *Thunderbolt* remained on his feet. The ship lifted again, but not fast enough to keep a green wave from crashing down on her and sweeping the length of her upper deck. Blade felt himself being stretched out by the tug of the water like a man on the rack and saw half a dozen men with a less iron grip than his go sailing over the side with despairing cries. The ship lifted and surged forward. Then she struck again, harder, and a third time, harder still.

At the third shock, Blade felt the whole ship strain and then sag and, looking aft, he saw the deck already beginning to buckle. Some submerged rock had driven up through *Thunderbolt's* bottom, snapping the keel like a twig and impaling the whole ship like a butterfly on a pin. She was still rising and falling as the waves surged under her, and the grinding and splintering as her timbers began to pull apart rose to equal the thunder of the waves.

Looking forward, Blade saw that by a small piece of good fortune, they were less than a hundred yards from a sandy beach. But by a larger piece of bad fortune, most of that hundred yards was a spouting cauldron of foam as the waves broke and died on a maze of submerged rocks. Blade could see sullen gray and black masses looming amid the white. But *Thunderbolt* would carry them no farther. It was time to rely on their own muscles. Blade looked at Tuabir, who nodded, then stepped forward and shouted over the wind:

"All hands, prepare to abandon ship!"

Most of the pirates could swim. For those who couldn't, Blade and Brora took axes from the carpenter's stores and began chopping out pieces of the railing. But whether swimmers or non-swimmers, they were all hanging back,

100

as though hoping that somehow there would be some alternative to plunging into the angry water.

Blade would have gone first, to show that it could be done. But he felt himself to be in a sense the Captain and therefore by the tradition of the seas (both here and Home Dimension's) the last man off. He did not have to wait long, however. Brora laid down his axe, raised his hand in salutation to Blade and Tuabir, then tied the rope around his waist and the other end firmly to the mast. He turned, quickly took the three steps to the side, and plunged over.

No one aboard *Thunderbolt* moved. All were too intent on watching for the small, dark shape of Brora's head to reappear amid the flurries of white as the line ran out. Then a cheer, as not only Brora's head but half his upper body rose to view on the crest of a breaker, arms moving strongly. Then it sank from sight, rose again, sank, remained out of sight a long time—then suddenly a small, dark figure was staggering up out of the water onto the beach, the foam curling about his legs. They saw him sit down, then untie the rope from around his waist and retie it around a nearby boulder. He got to his feet again and raised his arms in a beckoning gesture.

That started the men moving, finally. One by one, they stepped to the side, slipped into the water, and groped for the rope. As more and more weight came on it, Blade saw it tighten like a bowstring. But it held, and soon the first men to go were joining Brora on the shore. A few heroic souls promptly stepped back into the water, forming a human chain reaching out to help their shipmates ashore.

Not every man made it. Too often those aboard saw bobbing heads and flailing arms swept away from the rope, as the men were pulled loose by the strength of the sea. Closer to shore, they smashed against the rocks as the rope fell and rose with the ship's motion.

In a time almost too short for Blade to believe, *Thunderbolt's* deck was deserted except for him and Tuabir. Just as well. The ship was slipping deeper in the water each time a wave surged past and dropped her. Green water flowed over the deck a foot deep each time a wave rose up under her. Tuabir turned to Blade and said,

"Master Blahyd? You're the rightful Captain, but might I ask that I be last off the old lady? I've sailed aboard her twelve years now."

Blade nodded. The old sailor wanted to say goodbye to his ship, and Blade could hardly refuse. They shook hands, and Blade turned to face the water. He took a long running step, sprang, and plunged cleanly over the side into the sea.

Instantly the surge had him, but the rope was there, rasping against his side even through his shirt. He clutched at it with both hands, raised his head to get his bearings as a wave lifted him, then began pulling himself along the rope like a monkey. Sometimes a wave roared over him, pressing him down into the murky water until it seemed that his lungs would burst before he had a chance to breathe again. Sometimes he soared up on top of a wave until his arms practically pulled free of their sockets as he struggled to hold on. Foot by foot, the distance to shore shrank.

In one moment, he felt the bottom come up and slam hard against his legs, then the whole rope vibrated and he felt it go slack. Then there was a tingling boil of foam, as a receding wave collided with an advancing one. He was thrown forward, turned a complete somersault, then crashed down again, feet towards the land. With every bit of his colossal strength he lunged forward and staggered to his feet. Behind him the roar of another wave was building. He could stand up now, and so ran forward, ignoring the hands outstretched to help him. He didn't let his legs stop pushing him forward until he felt sand and grass under his feet; then he sat down and looked back toward *Thunderbolt*.

She had tilted over far enough to snap the rope. Blade saw the water rushing in and out of the splintered gashes in her hull. On the foc's'le was a solitary black figure. Tuabir. Blade waved frantically to the man, and thought he saw an answer. Then *Thunderbolt* sagged apart in the middle, plunging bow and stern deep into the water just as a wave struck. Blade saw timbers and foam rocket into the air, but the figure was gone. Blade turned away while

102

his seawater laden stomach rebelled. When he looked back to the sea, *Thunderbolt* was gone also, and only the black shapes of scattered timbers remained, tossing their way toward the shore.

Brora's voice called his attention back to the land. He looked up. A double file of armed men was curling its way down the path from the top of the bluff toward them. They were armed in what Blade had heard described as the style of Royth—plate cuirasses, square wooden shields, swords and throwing pikes. But on the shields was the silver bear on the blue field of Count Indhios.

Blade heard Alixa gasp and saw her point to the men with a shaking finger and heard Brora curse. The rest of the men knew nothing about the affair of Indhios and what his device on the shields of the approaching men might mean, but they silently turned their heads to look.

As if in response to Alixa's gesture, the company commander halted his men some thirty feet away and dressed their lines. He himself stepped out in front and shouted at the pirates, his words coming raggedly against the wind:

"By the laws of the Kingdom of Royth and by the authority invested in me by the Lord of Grand Ayesh, the Count Indhios, High Chancellor of the Realm, and—" He lost the thread of his remarks and mumbled for a moment. This drew a laugh from the pirates. Then he recovered himself and went on. "By these I declare that you, being notorious pirates of Neral now under the authority of the King of Royth, shall at once forfeit your lives if you do not submit peacefully." He turned to his men and motioned. The rasp of swords being drawn came clearly to Blade's ears.

The pirates were outnumbered nearly two to one, more in that some were wounded and all were exhausted, and had nothing but their daggers. Still, Blade heard a growl behind him as the pirates rose to their feet and faced the soldiers. He shook his head sharply. A fight would be suicide for all of them—and against soldiers in the pay of Indhios might also lead to Alixa's being "accidentally" killed. He stepped forward.

"We are forswearing the Brotherhood, Captain. I—"

103

"I have no authority to accept pirates into pardon, man," said the captain crisply. "Now—will your ruffians disarm, or shall I order the advance?" And he cast an unmistakable look of recognition at Alixa.

Blade drew his dagger, held it for a moment while he glared at the captain, then threw it point down into the sand. Behind him, the pirates did the same. As the soldiers advanced, pulling ropes from their belts to bind the prisoners, Blade stood rocklike, cursing savagely under his breath. They had managed a desperately dangerous voyage in safety, then thrown it all away trying to reach a port where Indhios would not find it easy to reach them. Tuabir and a third of the crew were dead, and after all of it here they had stepped straight into Indhios' hands, as if they had steered straight up to his private landing place. It was a damnable irony, and might rapidly become much worse.

CHAPTER 14

Things did not get too much worse immediately. After a night spent huddled in an empty warehouse at the local army camp, where they were fed, the prisoners began the march across the island. That took the better part of two days. After the wild crossing to the mainland, there followed seven more days of continuous marching before they reached High Royth, the capital.

It was on this march that things became grim. Some of the pirates died of exhaustion or exposure or collapsed and were finished off by the soldiers. Blade, however, kept stubbornly on, putting one foot in front of another with dogged determination. He also kept eyes and ears open, and as a result learned much.

Indhios' influence was still on the increase. He had been awarded the lordship of the Ayesh Islands (including the job of protecting them from pirate raids) barely three months ago. This latest plum was for divers and sundry

104

services in increasing and ordering the revenues of the Kingdom. Judging from the state of the villages along the road, Blade suspected that Indhios' methods involved mainly bleeding the peasants and tradesmen white. Moreover, judging from the size of the escort and of the camps on Grand Ayesh, the money Indhios was bleeding off was going more to build his private army than to increase the royal revenue. The Chancellor was already far too strong for comfort and getting stronger every day.

In an odd way, the fact that Indhios' soldiers had arrested them as pirates was slightly reassuring. If they had simply been turned loose, it would have suggested that Indhios now felt himself able to openly befriend the pirates. The Chancellor apparently did not yet feel strong enough to abandon *all* pretense of being a loyal servant of the Crown. Blade wondered, however, whether after the pirates marched into High Royth, the next thing to happen might be an invitation for him to visit the Chancellor. From his extensive, if reluctantly acquired experience of intrigue, he wouldn't have been surprised.

However, nothing like that happened. On a gray, snowy day, the thirty-five ragged and bloody-footed survivors of *Thunderbolt's* crew limped in through the West Gate of High Royth, across the Central Bridge, and into the citadel. There Blade and Brora were separated from the rest of the crew and given the dubious privilege of a cell of their own.

Blade was now becoming something of a connoisseur of odd places of confinement, and except for the Official Secrets Act might have written a book called *Strange Prisons I Have Known*. The dungeon in Royth had nothing unusual about it, being dark, damp, miserably cold, and moderately infested with assorted insects. However, neither he nor Brora were chained, and the food, if barely edible, was at least regular.

Apart from the twice-daily food and water, the two men were left alone with the vermin and the dampness for nearly two weeks. The enforced leisure gave Blade ample opportunity to try to make his own plans.

He was settling down to his fifteenth night on the

105

moldy straw when the rattling of keys being turned in the lock and the rusty squeal of the door being opened jerked him out of his doze. "Uh, Cap'n, some'un here to take you w' him," grunted the guard. Behind the too-familiar figure of the guard, a small, slender figure in dark red was visible. Who was it? Not Alixa—she was much taller than that. Not Indhios—not if the Chancellor was as fat as described. Possibly a messenger, and if so, whose? Had Indhios finally decided to pay some attention to him? If so, he might be on his way to a dangerous interview. If Indhios got one inkling of his plans to carry on Khystros' work, the man would hardly balk at having him killed without delay.

He wrapped his blanket, his only garment since his sailor's clothes had fallen apart, around himself, and stepped through the door. The figure in red beckoned to him without a word. The hand that beckoned was small, but gloved, and gave no clue as to its owner's sex or age.

Whoever the person in red was, they had apparently done a remarkably thorough job of ordering, intimidating, or bribing the guards. None of them turned a hair at seeing the huge Blade striding down the corridors free of all restraints, his bare chest and wildly tangled hair and beard making him look even more formidable than usual.

Blade had no very good idea of the inner layout of the citadel, but he was surprised that his guide did not turn upward along any of the numerous stairways. Instead, they kept on through progressively lower and lower and darker and darker corridors, until Blade realized they must now be well outside the walls of the citadel. He saw racks of old armor lurking in shadowy alcoves, with vast festoons of cobwebs hanging from them, and rats scurrying red-eyed and nimble-footed around them.

The long prowl through underground passages finally ended when they came to what appeared to Blade as a blank wall. But the same small gloved hand now reached out and pushed firmly against the stone. With a faint rumble, an entire section of the wall pivoted around on a central spindle, opening on a narrow flight of stairs leading up into total darkness. Reluctantly, Blade followed his

106

guide. Underground warrens put him in mind of Cayla and her nightmare shrines, and he began to wonder whether the guide might not be another of the Serpent Priestesses.

But when they reached the end of the long stairs and stepped out through another pivoted door, it was into a circular room whose narrow slitted windows looked out on the rooftops and streets of High Royth from a height of nearly a hundred feet. This was some castle tower, and the castle of some high person in the Kingdom, judging from the richness of the furnishings. A great bed, with hangings and quilts in the same shade of red as his guide's robes, stood in the middle of the room. The floor was covered by carpets of the same color and the walls by heavy tapestries in which reds, oranges, and yellows dominated the patterns. Even the candles that hung in red copper lanterns from the walls were red and burned with a reddish light.

For a moment Blade was so absorbed in trying to guess the nature of the room's occupant from the clues offered by its furnishings that he paid no attention to the other person with him. In that moment, the small figure in red stepped up to him and deftly whipped the blanket away.

Blade was only startled, for he was twice the size of the other. If it came to a fight, he had nothing to fear, even in his weakened condition. However, he thought it was time to ask a few questions.

"Who are you?"

The laugh that escaped from behind the red veil was unmistakably feminine, and Blade relaxed somewhat. The voice replied with a question of its own. "Can't you think of a more original question, oh great and wise pirate Captain?"

"I can't think of any I want answered as badly," he replied shortly."

"Ah, well," she said, and drew her gloves off, then lifted her hands—fine, delicate ones, Blade noted—to the veil and hood and pulled both away.

The face that looked out at him was marvelously beautiful and delicately wrought. Everything seemed sculptured from a material so fragile that to touch it or even breathe on it would make it crumple. The hair that framed the face was glossy and intensely brown, with a reddish tinge that might have been its own, or given it by the light in the rom. And the large eyes that were roving over Blade's body held an expression that he knew extremely well. He hoped that nothing more was involved here than simple lust. That he felt perfectly willing and able to gratify. He viewed with much less enthusiasm the idea of involvement in more plots, particularly those of the Serpent Priestesses.

The lady clearly had her mind on other things than answering Blade's questions and at once set out to make sure that his mind would not be on asking any. She knelt before him, her mouth open and her mobile lips already moving in hungry anticipation, and set to work on him. It did not take long to fully arouse him, for it was a skilled mouth as well as a mobile one. With only minor pauses in her work, the lady unfastened the clasp of her cloak, then her robe. Both slipped to the floor. Under them she wore a filmly red gown, and under that Blade could see the outlines of her body. It matched her face in its exquisite delicacy.

He reached out his hands and pressed both of them into her mass of dark brown hair. The gesture made her look up. "Yes, you are becoming impatient, great Captain. And you are *great*." She made an explicit gesture in the appropriate direction. "Come, then." She led him over to the bed and motioned him to lie back on the quilts. Then quickly she jerked the red gown over her head and mounted him.

Her body was as perfect as he had anticipated, with small, brown-nippled breasts whose slight sag suggested that she was perhaps not as young as he had believed. But there was not an ounce of excess fat in all her delicate and graceful curves as she writhed and wriggled and drove herself down on him again and again. It seemed that they would go on until their bodies melted and ran together like ice cream on a hot day, but at last Blade felt the end of his control approaching. He fought to hold back as

108

long as possible, but in the end he spurted furiously into her, and his spasm touched off hers.

She lay atop him for a long time after collapsing, her eyes closed and her furious breathing gradually subsiding to normal. Then her eyes opened and she grinned—an impish grin that at once took Blade back to the notion of her as a girl barely out of her teens.

"I," she said, "am the Countess Indhios. But the name for you to use is Larina."

It was a while before Blade felt he could safely reply to that remark. Then he said, "The Count has a most beautiful and accomplished lady."

She grimaced. "The pretty speeches are for before, not after. And for us, not at all. If I thought you needed them, you would still be in the dungeon."

Blade kept silent. This was another decisive, almost dictatorial woman. She was like Cayla in that way; he hoped it was *only* in that way. Then, swiftly, in the same soft voice, she demolished his previous hopes that here at least were no plots.

She knew of her husband's plans to betray Royth to the pirates. He did not completely trust her, but on the other hand, he was too vain to pass up the chance of having someone to boast to. He would kill her in a moment if he suspected betrayal, but so far he suspected nothing.

Why was she betraying his plans? King Pelthros was a widower and childless. Now that Grand Duke Khystros was dead, there was no heir the King really trusted. He might well contemplate re-marrying—a younger woman, who could bear him children, particularly if that woman had rendered some signal service to the Kingdom.

"Such as revealing Indhios' plans?"

"Indeed."

"Causing Indhios' prompt execution, and leaving you a young widow."

"Exactly."

"But—" She took his "but" for disapproval, and snapped:

"I have no love for Indhios. There is nothing between us but our two children. And how much trouble it was to

109

get him to my bed often enough for those, I could take ten nights telling you. He married me for my dowry, then repaid my father for his generosity by levying such taxes on his lands that he is now ground down to the level of his own peasants. Indhios' lusts are for power and gold, not the clean lusts of men for women."

That was the Countess' grand design. As for Blade's specific part in it, she needed a man with a martial reputation and a position at Court that enabled him to move about freely. She needed a combined spy and bravo, and if he were also a fit and proper bedmate, so much the better. Before Blade had any time to wonder how he, an imprisoned pirate Captain, was going to attain such a position at Court, she swept on to the next detail of her plan.

"A most ancient law of the Kingdom of Royth declares that any man, whatever his blood or birth, who comes before the Court and challenges the King's Champion may meet him in equal combat to the death. If victorious, he shall then swear oath of fealty to the King and become in his turn King's Champion. Centuries ago, the King's Champion had many duties that often called upon his martial prowess, so it was needful to select only the best fighters to serve the Kings so. But now, the King's Champion is more for show than for service, like a suit of gilded armor set with jewels. But he still stands high at Court, has access to the King, and may move about freely." Blade nodded. He could see what was coming.

"I have heard much of your prowess with weapons and would be much astonished if you could not spit Baron Maltravos, the Champion of the moment, like a cook spitting a goose. Then you will be King's Champion, to watch over King Pelthros—and those about him. You shall seek out those details of his schemes which Indhios will not reveal even to me when boasting in his cups. You shall bring them to me, and then when the time is ripe we shall lay all we have both learned before Pelthros and bring Indhios' schemes crashing about his head. Pelthros is a slow man to reach a decision, preferring too much his crafts to the business of a king. But the royal house of

110

Royth has yet to breed an utter fool. Pelthros will see what is thrust in front of his nose."

"Will Indhios let me challenge and fight the Champion?"

"Pelthros will enforce the ancient law if you can safely make your way into the Court. Indhios can do nothing then. But he will kill you if he can reach you before you reach the Court. He knows of your plans to carry on Khystros' work."

That was no great surprise to Blade. It was certainly the most reasonable explanation of his confinement in the dungeon. "How did Indhios find out?"

"Alixa."

Blade sat up violently, but Larina pressed a hand to his chest. "No, it is not what you think. She did not betray you. Indhios took her under his 'protection.' Then he gave her wine mixed with herbs that make a person unable to lie. She answered his questions because she had no will to do otherwise."

It seemed to Blade that the countess was indifferent to his relationship with Alixa, but then why *should* she be jealous? She was aiming far higher. She could find use for Blade as a bed partner, to be sure, but her plans would not be affected by this one way or another.

Again, Blade faced making a major decision in a few seconds. And again, he decided to acquiesce. If there was a better way out of the dungeons of Royth than through the countess' plans, he had not heard of it. Nor would it be wise to wait around in hope that one might turn up. If Indhios was on his trail, he was in deadly danger while locked in the citadel. The same guards that had been bribed to let the countess through to release him might also be bribed to let Indhios or one of his assassins through to kill him. And there were other useful things that could come from joining the countess.

"What about my crew?"

"You wish to protect them from the King's justice?"

Blade's voice would have risen to a shout if he had let it. "Damn you, they are my men! They forswore their oaths to the Brotherhood of Neral to follow me here, and

111

more than half their shipmates are drowned or dead on the road because of me. If you won't help me take them out of their dungeon, then at least let me go back to mine!"

Larina drew back and raised herself on one elbow to look at him. "You are a strange man, Blahyd. Almost like one of the ancient heroes. They too would die rather than betray their followers. Yes, I think you will draw much attention as King's Champion if you speak then as you speak now."

Blade would not be turned from his subject by fuzzily worded flattery. "My crew's pardon. Or find somebody else to help you climb over your husband's body to the throne of Royth!" For a moment, he wondered if he had gone too far. She might now suspect that he would be too independent to be a good ally and take him at his word.

Then she nodded. "I will let certain people know that your crew genuinely wishes to be admitted to pardon. That will at least put off their trial and execution, which otherwise Indhios would not delay. But you can do the most for them yourself by becoming the new King's Champion. When you stand forth above Baron Maltravos' body, King Pelthros will grant almost any request you may ask of him. Only—you must win!"

Then she turned to him, and her skilled hands and lips began their work once more. Before his arousal put an end to his thinking, it occurred to Blade that there were now no less than five different plots all focusing on the Kingdom of Royth. There was Indhios' scheme. There was that of the Council of Captains and the Neralers generally. There was Cayla's monstrous notion of a revival of the Serpent Cult. There was the ambitious and ruthless little countess. Each of these four would cheerfully sell any or all of the others to the devil to get them out of the way. And there was his own comparatively simple plan, to save Royth from the pirates. But was this decadent and ancient land worth the effort? And even if it was worth the effort, would he live long enough to carry his efforts through?

CHAPTER 15

Blade was uncomfortably aware that winter would not last forever, so he became increasingly impatient as he endured day after day of luxurious imprisonment in Larina's red-hung tower chamber. It was not until the eleventh day after his release from the dungeon that the countess appeared with two servants. They were apparently deaf mutes, and they brought a complete suit of Court attire, as well as Blade's own battered but familiar weapons.

She also brought him unwelcome news that made him even happier that the time to make his move had come. "My husband is determined to keep control of Alixa. Tonight he will petition the King to make her his ward. If this is granted, he will find it easy to kill her. Or he may merely plunder her fortune and turn the girl herself over to the pirates for their amusement when they have taken the Kingdom." That probably meant Alixa would end up in Cayla's hands, Blade knew. So he was aggressively ready for fast and bloody action when the countess led him up the steps of the palace and through the high-arched entry hall into the Grand Court Chamber. The palace was a sprawling jumble of buildings of all eras and styles jammed together cheek-by-jowl, the whole ensemble coated with a fine patina of moss and age. It was at once magnificent and shabby. The air inside hung heavy in Blade's nostrils with the odors of mold and dampness and ancient filth lurking in remote corners.

"Remember," she whispered in his ear before drifting away to join her husband in the line of notables flanking the throne, "no outbursts, whatever Indhios does. And no signals to Alixa. The count can still have you slain at any moment before you step forward and issue the challenge. So when you do do that, do it quickly, so that the law may be invoked before Indhios can react."

Blade nodded and adjusted the scarf that concealed

most of his face. He wore it because, as the countess had told the bewigged Chamberlain, it hid a healing battle wound which yet made his face a thing too unsightly for the eyes of gentlefolk. He would discard it of course when he issued his challenge. But for now it kept him concealed from prying eyes among the five hundred or so gorgeously dressed men and women that drifted about the vast domed chamber. Like the palace, their finery often seemed out of phase with itself and reeking of age.

The ceiling rose so high that the vaulting was almost lost in shadow, and the massive block of green marble that supported the twin thrones seemed shrunken and diminished. It was a room that seemed designed as a meeting place of elderly giants. There was no way for it to seem appropriate for the stout, gray-haired man in the fur-trimmed dark blue robe who suddenly stepped out of a shadowed doorway to quietly walk up onto the dais and sit down on the right-hand throne. It took the Chamberlain's bark and the clatter as the soldiers came to attention to make Blade realize that here at last was King Pelthros.

There was a great rustling of rich fabrics as the five hundred men and women suddenly froze in midstep and went down on one knee, heads turned toward the King. Pelthros spread his arms wide, and as the company rose, nodded to his Herald.

Blade, waiting with ever increasing impatience and watching the countess for her signal, saw one trivial person after another announced by the Herald, amble up, and present their even more trivial items of business. Most of them mumbled or stammered so that Blade could barely make out every third word. He doubted that he was missing a great deal.

But when he saw Indhios lead Alixa forward, pale and trembling and looking small beside the enormous swollen bulk of the count, his hand quietly drifted toward his sword hilt. It took a great deal of self-control for him to stand quietly and listen to Indhios presenting his petition and almost more than he had when he saw Pelthros nod and Indhios lead Alixa away and give her into the guard of one of his henchmen.

114

The girl had just vanished, and Blade had just turned his eyes back to the throne, when a flicker of motion caught his attention. He turned, saw the countess raising her white-gloved hand to her ear and patting the rich curls just behind it into position. He grinned savagely. It was time.

Blade loomed half a head over most of the men as he strode forward, the plain, battle-worn sword gleaming at his side a vivid contrast to the jeweled weapons of the courtiers. He kept straight on through the crowd until he was less than twenty feet from the throne, bowed, and with a theatrical sweep of one powerful arm tore away the red scarf.

Pelthros' eyes opened, and as Blade rose and turned, a general gasp arose from the crowd, accompanied by a rasp of drawn swords. The guards came to attention, but yet made no move to step between him and the King. Pelthros cleared his throat, keeping (Blade noticed) a firm grip on the hilt of his own sword, and said, "So Captain Blahyd, the pirate of Neral, has somehow contrived to come to our Court. What brings you before us?"

"Your Majesty, I claim a right according to the ancient law of your mighty Kingdom. To fight in equal battle against your Champion, and if victorious, to swear fealty to you and stand in his place until another come and prove himself superior in the same way." Blade had rehearsed getting his request out in a brief but formal speech over and over again. It was just as well, because Indhios lumbered forward wasting no time in spluttering indignantly, his voice rising to a roar.

"Your Majesty!" he bellowed. "This man is the leader of a band of Neraler pirates of the worst sort. They were shipwrecked on the coast of Grand Ayesh, which Your Majesty had most graciously given into my—"

"Silence!" thundered Pelthros, rising from the throne and to Blade's surprise easily outbellowing his Chancellor. "The law says that if a man steps forward and offers challenge to the King's Champion, that challenge must be accepted. It is indeed an ancient law of this Realm, as the Captain says, nor shall it be abridged while we sit upon

115

the throne of Royth." Blade had to admit that in spite of all that he had heard against the man, Pelthros could at least act like a king when necessary. In fact, Indhios was backing away like a bear backing away from a hunter.

The silence the King had demanded had fallen like a foot of snow over the gathering, chilling and stifling conversation. All eyes were on Blade now, until the King raised his voice again and called, "Herald, summon the King's Champion!"

But Baron Maltravos was already pushing his way forward through the crowd of notables flanking the thrones. Blade took the chance to size up the man as he strode out into the clear space in front of the throne and bowed with a graceful arrogance that was almost contemptuous of both the King and the whole Court. Shorter than Blade by half a head, but with long arms and legs supporting a squat, broad torso, there was something apelike about him. But there was no apish deviltry in the gray eyes staring out of a face half swallowed up in bristling beard, only a cold sizing up of Blade in return. Blade's trained judgment made its assessment and passed him its opinion: this was a dangerous man. He would be fast, he would have great endurance, and he would have against him only Blade's great size and his own over-confidence. The baron's words confirmed the judgment:

"Well, Your Majesty, do we need to waste your gracious time and that of your loyal subjects any further? I see that the Neraler wretch comes armed. I say, let me kill him now, and have done with it." And he whipped from their scabbards a broadsword and a shortsword and made both of them blur and whistle in the air.

"I will fight as the baron wishes," said Blade. "But might I ask for a shield?" The King nodded and beckoned to one of the guards, who ran forward and handed Blade his own shield, a circle of leather over wood about two and a half feet across, with a bronze rim and a bronze boss at the center. Blade hefted it a few times to judge its weight and carefully flexed his muscles to loosen them. The baron watched with an open sneer twisting his face, visible even through the beard.

The Herald raised his hand, trumpets blared from the alcoves, and the crowd of courtiers and their ladies gave back hastily, leaving free a circle some thirty feet in diameter in front of the throne. That, Blade recalled, was exactly the same size as the arena in which Cayla had slaughtered Dynera. But instead of ropes tied to oars, this arena was marked off by a ring of royal guards, glowering impartially outward at the courtiers and inward at the two fighters standing in the middle.

The audience was silent. Blade could not read their expressions clearly enough to guess if they were going to prove partisan, and if so, for whom. Nor was it important. A cheering section will not revive a corpse.

Blade had never fought before against the formal two-swords style that Maltravos was apparently planning to use, except in the Medieval Club at Oxford. But that little experience had taught him that it was deadly for a man with the speed and coordination to use it. A weapon in either hand gave the fighter an extra offensive punch, and if he chose to use both for defense, he could raise an almost unbreakable wall of steel between him and the opponent.

The baron moved forward, shortsword held out in the guard position and broadsword raised for an overhand stroke. Blade moved in himself, saw the broadsword whirl toward his head, jerked his shield up in time to catch the stroke, then pulled it down as the shortsword stabbed toward his groin. He braced his feet apart, swung his own sword, and saw the baron whip both of his weapons up into an X-pattern that caught Blade's descending stroke neatly in the upper fork of the X. Blade nearly had his sword wrenched out of his hand as the baron sidestepped, disengaged, and came in again.

In a matter of the few seconds it took for half a dozen more exchanges of blows, Blade realized he was going to have to fight for his life and worry about victory later, if at all. The baron's broadsword whistled over his head and past his ear by hair-thin margins or crashed deafeningly against the top and edge of his shield. The shortsword flickered like a striking snake toward belly, groin, and thigh. His own slashes clanged off the baron's guard, and

117

his own thrusts were always beaten down by one of the baron's whistling strokes. The man was every bit as fast as he was, Blade realized. And unlike Oshawal, he might have equal or greater endurance.

Back and forth across the circle they sprang in a continuous fury of exchanges, broken only by momentary pauses when by mutual if unspoken consent they drew apart to wipe their faces free of the sweat now flooding down their bodies and darkening their tunics and breeches. Then they would return to the battle.

Blade was conscious of mutterings and murmurings among the crowd now, as people noted the fine points of each fighter's techniques or gasped at some particularly hairbreadth escape—usually one of his. The baron might as well have been a machine, for all the strain he was showing. Blade, however, was becoming conscious of rasping breath and rubbery legs and arms as his prison-weakened frame began to rebel against the burden falling on it. But he at least could see in his opponent's eyes the dying of the former arrogant confidence and the beginning of—not fear, but at least strain and uncertainty. The baron began to use strokes designed to kill, not merely to show off his prowess in handling his swords.

A moment came, twenty minutes (though feeling more like twenty years) into the fight. The baron sprang out of a resting guard, feinting with the broadsword and thrusting with the shortsword in the same split second. Blade half-crouched, feeling the wind of the broadsword above his head—and feeling the point of the shortsword wedge itself for a moment in one of the gashes that scarred the surface of his shield. In the extra fraction of a second the baron needed to jerk his shortsword free and begin to back away, Blade drove his own sword forward in a lightning thrust and saw the point rake along Maltravos' left forearm and sink deep into his bicep. The blood welled up fast.

Blade felt an inner surge of new strength as the baron sprang clear, staring at his arm. And he felt the mood of the crowd swing in his favor—or was it just in favor of blood and victory, no matter whose? No time to think that over now, only time to press his advantage. He stepped up his own pace to a level he knew he could not maintain for long, and pressed his attack.

In another minute the baron showed blood on the side of his neck and a moment after that on his left thigh. But although he had abandoned the furious offensive of the first stages of the fight, he was still maintaining a solid defense. Blade heard the crowd, for a few moments perhaps his partisans, subside once again into rumblings and occasional remarks. And he knew he was pouring the last of his strength into an offense that had yet to break decisively through to the baron. He would have to draw the baron out, and soon.

As he stepped back for a moment's break, his opponent did not let him move away unmolested. Instead Maltravos sprang out of his defensive stance with both swords slicing the air. Blade gave way before the attack, put his left foot into a slick smear of blood on the floor, and felt himself going over backward.

Instantly the reflexes developed by his unarmed combat training took over. Before he hit the ground he had whipped his left arm forward to hurl the shield at the baron and lashed out with his right foot at the baron's kneecap. Both strokes connected. It was the baron's turn to reel back so violently that he lost his balance. Blade continued his backward fall, kicked himself over into a complete backward somersault, and came up still clutching his sword before the baron had regained his feet. For a moment the solid defense was shattered. Blade thrust with every ounce of strength and speed he had left, saw his point drive through Maltravos' chest, heard it scrape on the floor as it came out Maltravos' back. Blood came out of the baron's mouth, he coughed twice, then his grip on his swords relaxed and they clattered to the floor on either side of their dead master.

Blade felt like falling forward and lying face down on the stone until his head stopped whirling. Instead, he pulled his sword free, laid it down beside his shield, and turned to the King.

119

"Is it Your Majesty's judgment that I defeated Baron Maltravos in equal and fair combat?"

There was a moment's silence while the King pulled at his beard and another, deeper silence fell over the crowd. Then he looked at Blade, smiled, and said:

"You have, Captain Blahyd. And so be it. Herald, proclaim the new Champion of the King of Royth!"

As the trumpets blared again and the crowd swept the guards aside to cluster round him and congratulate him, Blade's legs finally gave under him and he sank to the floor not far from the baron's body. Part of his mind was hurling sharp remarks at him for this weakness, reminding him that his crew still needed protection and much else had to be done. The other part was informing him that he was not far from collapse and that if he had in truth any influence as Champion, it would not vanish in the few minutes it took to restore a small fraction of his energy. Eventually, he got his legs moving again and, half-walking, half-stumbling, he made his way out of the Court chamber in the wake of two guards assigned to lead him to his new quarters. The last things he saw before passing through the high-arched door with its bronze grill folded back were the faces of Alixa and the countess. They were staring at him from opposite sides of the room, and both had a combination of awe and hope in their eyes.

CHAPTER 16

Blade soon discovered that while being King's Champion of Royth got him and his crew out of prison, it did not immediately solve very many of his other problems. Brora and the other pirates went through a solemn and humiliating ceremony at the local temple of Druk and, after being pronounced cleansed of the taint of the Brotherhood, went to work in the royal dockyards. Blade had a chance for a few words with Brora before the sailor led his men off to their new work.

"Find out who in the dockyards supports Indhios and who opposes him. If you can safely do so, organize the ones on our side for action in a crisis. They may be needed." Brora nodded and went off without a word. Blade knew the man understood him perfectly and would do as much as humanly possible to win over and organize the dockyard workers.

Brora and the others at least had the consolation of hard, useful work day in and day out. For Blade, the duty of King's Champion proved to entail more show than work, as the countess had warned him it would. It gave him the freedom of movement he needed to play his role in his own (and Larina's) intrigues, and to visit Larina herself occasionally. But otherwise it was a thoroughgoing bore. For Blade it had more and more of a bird-in-a-gilded-cage feeling as the weeks wore on.

And also, as the weeks wore on the winter chill faded from the winds, and buds began to appear on the trees. Blade became more and more impatient. What he had learned in Royth confirmed what he had picked up in Neral—this was the year Indhios would make his move. And the year was pushing onward to the moment when Indhios would be prepared to strike.

Larina drove him wild with frustration as she continued to turn aside all his urgings for quick action, saying that while he might be a fighting man, *she* knew the intrigues of the Court. It would be folly to risk everything by moving prematurely. Blade was equally convinced it was becoming folly to wait, risking discovery by the Chancellor.

Blade was also becoming more concerned about Alixa. She was still in High Royth, or so it was reported, but any day now the Chancellor might decide to send her to one of his more remote estates, where she could be kept safely for the day when she would be turned over to the pirates. Even if Indhios himself were caught, it would be an easy thing for his henchmen to use Alixa as a hostage for their own escape, and tracking down every one of Indhios' agents would be impossible. Only a quick blow at the count and his leading allies together, beheading thc whole conspiracy at one stroke, stood any chance of saving

121

Royth. And apart from that, Blade wanted Alixa safe. In this intrigue-riddled Dimension, she was one of the few whole, sound, sane people he had found. Still, for all the countess' assurances that she was not jealous of Alixa, Blade could not quite trust her reaction if he urged faster action because it would help to save Alixa.

The winds grew warmer still; dawn now came before Blade slipped from Larina's bed and down the stairs to where his horse waited. The buds began to turn to young leaves, and on a blue sea the white, red, and brown sails of ships began to appear. The seas were opening again—to pirates as well as peaceful commerce.

Brora's talents and his previous reputation and popularity had led to his being given full charge of a dock, with the rank of an officer. Most of the other ex-pirates, except for a few incorrigibles, had also done well, in spite of the prejudice against even forsworn Neralers. Brora and his men had learned much and were learning more.

A fair number of the officers of the dockyard and the fleet had gone over to Indhios, who was pouring out money and promises with a lavishness that Blade knew could not be long maintained. These formed a solid, well-organized bloc. There was a smaller group, with some officers but mostly led by the senior warrant officers, foremen and the like, who were sworn to fight Indhios and his allies to the death. These had already done much to organize for action even before Brora appeared. And as always, there was the majority of both officers and men who saw nothing beyond their daily jobs and knew little and cared less of politics.

There was an extensive district of cheap waterfront taverns and sailors' dives where most of the plotting and counterplotting went on. There Blade and Brora met every few nights to exchange information over leather cups of sour wine and scummy beer. Blade disliked the smells of overaged fish cooked in rancid oil, the guttering torchlight, the shrill-voiced trulls and snarling tavernkeepers that filled the area, but it was by far the best place to meet in safety. Indhios had few if any supporters among the tavern population, and some of those who had been incautious enough to reveal themselves at the wrong time had never been seen again. Besides, Brora had a full twelve-hour day to work, while Blade had little or nothing to occupy his time except his occasional nights with Larina.

A gust-driven, spattering rain was falling on the huddled waterfront district as Blade made his way homeward toward the palace one night. This was a particularly bad area, and the night was warm, so he rode with his cloak thrown back and his sword openly exposed at his side. There was nothing to look forward to but the ceremonial good-night to the King and a late supper in the boring company of half a dozen other court functionaries, all of them twenty years older than he and with twenty years more of petty experiences to be boring about. The sigh and patter of the storm and the clop-clop of his horse's hooves were the only sounds.

Abruptly a cloaked figure slipped out from an alley to his left and darted at him. His sword was free in an instant, and he was flipping it up for a downstroke when the countess' voice spoke from inside the figure's hood:

"Blahyd! Abandon your horse—now!—and come with me!"

If it had been anybody else but the countess, Blade would have spurred the horse to a gallop and vanished up the hill. But though her presence here in this slum was a surprise, he knew the countess would not be here but for some good and important reason. She had too much common sense to risk herself unnecessarily. He felt the tingling and stimulation that the prospect of action often produced; he had not had a chance to feel this way for much too long.

The horse clattered away up the hill by itself and Blade followed the countess down a pitch-dark alley into a low-roofed shed. Four men, their faces darkened with soot, were sitting around a feeble oil lamp.

"My guards," said the countess. She turned to Blade and said, "Are your allies in the dockyards ready?"

Blade wanted to cheer out loud, but he only nodded and added, "As ready as they could be by now."

The countess smiled. "Well and good. Indhios plans to

123

move tomorrow night. His agents will start fires in the dockyards, destroying the navy's supplies and many warships. At the same time, others of his faction in the garrison will call out their troops to "suppress disorders" and will march on the palace. King Pelthros will be taken prisoner, drugged, and used as a puppet until the pirates arrive. And Indhios is sending Alixa up-country. She and her escort leave tonight."

Blade subdued a flare of rage at that news and asked, "Do you know the agents in the dockyard?"

She nodded and named several officers who were already on Brora's list, plus others Blade had not heard mentioned. "Let me write a note to Brora," he said, "and have one of your men take it to him immediately. He will probably still be at the Sailor's Friend on Brandy Street. That should be all we need to make the dockyard safe. Brora has little love for pirates." He quickly scribbled a few lines on a sheet of paper and folded it into a small square that one of the guards dropped into his pouch.

When the man had vanished into the night, the countess said, "For our part, it is time to go to the palace and alert the King. I have with me all the written evidence needed to convince even Pelthros, including your notes from your stay on Neral."

"How did you get those? I thought Indhios had them concealed safely."

"They were safe, until Indhios boasted too long to one of his henchmen. He no longer trusts me enough to speak before me, but his vanity has not changed. The man wanted me to come to his bed, and it was easy to raid his strongbox while he slept afterwards." She shivered with disgust at the memory. "Once we have Pelthros convinced, it should be easy. Indhios has only a few supporters among the courtiers, and I can rely on you to deal with them properly if they appear. The Royal Guard is mostly loyal to Pelthros. If they are alerted, they can easily defend the palace against Indhios' faction until the loyal troops come up. If we can only convince Pelthros and then keep him alive long enough to give the necessary orders . . ." Her jaw set, but her eyes were anything but

124

grim, gleaming with her own joy of battle and the hope of seeing her plans all come to fruition. "But we need no more talking. It is time to leave."

There were horses for all of them ready in a stable on the other side of the shed. As greatly as he wanted to break into a gallop, Blade kept his mount reined in to a trot all the way to the palace. It loomed high and somber in the night, with only the few gleams of light that marked the sentries' posts still breaking the darkness. As King's Champion, Blade could pass anywhere without question, even into the personal presence of the King with no permission other than the King's own. So the sentries at the outer gates passed them through without question once they recognized Blade.

Once inside, however, Blade kept his hand on his sword as they moved down the long, dark corridors towards the royal apartments. He cursed Pelthros' frugality that led to the palace being largely in darkness. If Indhios had any of his allies prowling in this darkness, they might have to fight their way through against men who knew the palace better than he did. Blade almost wanted to take off his boots and pad forward on his bare feet, as their footfalls echoed from the stone around them seemingly loud enough to shake the whole palace and wake the long-dead Kings of Royth in their tombs far below. But as they twisted and turned their way closer to their goal, the palace might still have been a city of the dead.

They saw nothing to start at but their own shadows when they passed through an area lighted by a feeble torch or a few candles and finally reached the small, square chamber that lay at the foot of the stairs leading to the actual private chambers of King Pelthros. Four soldiers were on duty in the chamber, tough young men in chased silver cuirasses and open-faced helms, officers from the elite Royal Guard. Now, though, the light of the bronze chandelier hanging from the roof of the chamber showed the hard, tanned faces as bored and inattentive as those of any sentry walking his post on a cold night in a rear-area garrison. One of them yawned in Blade's face as he led his party into the chamber.

125

Blade had no authority over the Royal Guard by law, but he had contrived friendships (or at least mutual trust) with some of the officers. Unfortunately, none of the ones he knew well were among the four on duty. The one who had yawned was a captain he knew only by name; the others he had never even seen.

"Good evening, Captain Tralthos."

"Morning, rather, Champion Blade. It's well on toward the second hour. What brings you here? And who are these people?"

"The Countess Indhios and three of her household." Tralthos' eyes widened at the name. "We have urgent business with His Majesty."

"Hand the message over and I'll see that it gets delivered to him the first thing in the morning," said Tralthos wearily.

"It must be delivered to His Majesty personally. And immediately."

Tralthos looked openly truculent. Blade could hardly blame the man. Or perhaps Indhios had managed to suborn some of the Palace Guard after all? A distinctly unpleasant thought. For a long moment Blade and Tralthos glared at each other in a direct confrontation of will power. At the end of that moment, it was Tralthos who gave way.

"All right," he grumbled, unable to manage his surrender with grace. "I'll go on up and wake the King."

"Do that," said Blade shortly. "And *hurry,* if you love your King!" He was feeling distinctly edgy. No premonitions of trouble—yet—but they could still be confounded and slain if a dozen of Indhios' bravos charged out of the darkness. He turned back to look at the long corridor. Nothing moved in it, out to the end of the torchlight where walls, floor, and ceiling all merged into blackness. Not yet.

Tralthos vanished up the stairs to the royal chambers. They saw his torch flicker its way up to the small door at the top, heard him knock, listened as he did for the response, then heard a door latch disengaged and a squeak of hinges as the door opened and he vanished through it.

126

Although they almost stopped breathing, in the vague murmur of words floating down the stairs to them they could still distinguish neither voices nor words. It occurred to Blade that it would be a monumental jest of the gods if the Kingdom of Royth were to fall to the Neraler pirates because its King objected to being awakened at two in the morning.

Then his speculation ended abruptly as Tralthos closed the door and came back down the stairs. "His Majesty will receive Champion Blade and the Countess Indhios, but the others must remain here." Blade nodded. "Also, you must leave your weapons down here."

Before Blade could explode in a futile and disastrous outburst of rage against all this timidity and bureaucracy, the countess laid a hand on his arm and said swiftly, "We agree. Lead us to the King," to Tralthos, and in a half-whisper to Blade, "Silence! Would you smash everything when we are so close?" Blade's temptation was to point out that they were not yet so close that they could not be interrupted—permanently—but Tralthos was already on his way back up the stairs and motioning them to follow him.

They found the King sitting on the edge of his bed, the blankets thrown back and the pillows shoved into a massive white pile in one corner. The bed itself was a huge canopied affair easily large enough to accommodate five people, hung with black brocade embroidered with red silk castles. Pelthros had pulled on a dark green chamber robe and belted his sword on over it. Otherwise he was barefoot, unkempt, with his thick salt-and-pepper beard and his not-so-thick gray hair sticking out in all directions, red-eyed and baleful in the glare he threw at the two visitors.

Blade let the countess explain their visit. She was more fluent in the Court formulas of speech, and had a strong personal incentive for making herself as conspicuous as possible in the King's eyes. Blade had no particular interest in politics any longer except insofar as it was necessary to convince Pelthros of the threat. After that, he wanted

127

only to work his way through the ranks of the enemy with his sword, starting with Indhios.

"Your Majesty," began the countess. "When your late brother, the Grand Duke Khystros, brought an accusation against Count Indhios, that the Chancellor was plotting to betray the Kingdom to the Neraler pirates, he spoke the truth." That, at least, gained her the King's attention. Then she moved into a rapid summary of what Indhios was plotting, what the pirates were plotting, who was allied with them—and how she and Blade had found out what they knew.

"And if you seek evidence that would stand before a Grand Court, then consider this—and this—and this," hauling notes and documents from the flowing sleeves of her gown. Blade could not help admiring the countess at this moment as she stood there, rendered formidable by her keen wits as well as by her beauty. If by some strange chain of events she did mount the throne of Royth beside Pelthros, then perhaps the Kingdom would finally have the political skill in high places that it so sadly lacked and so badly needed.

Pelthros remained silent and motionless, staring at the pile of documents she was laying beside him on the bed, either unable or unwilling to react. When the countess had finished and stepped back—almost posing, it struck Blade—the King raised his head and said:

"My Lady. If what you say is true, you are laying your husband's head on the block."

She sighed. It was a marvelously dramatic sigh. "I know that, Your Majesty. But—would you ask me to keep silent about such treason?" Her tone of voice was that of a person who has been driven after long hours of agonizing self-doubt to a yet more agonizing decision. It was also, it seemed to Blade, the tone of a person who hopes to see her remarks someday recorded in history books for the edification of children. If Blade had not known the quality of the mind behind this series of poses, he suspected he would have been either appalled or disgusted or both. As it was, the countess' acting was so splendid that Blade almost forgot the deadly stakes in the game they were playing.

Seconds later he was abruptly reminded of them. Feet clattered on the stairs and the door burst open so violently that it crashed against the wall. One of the countess' guards tumbled into the bedroom, gasping incoherently, blood pouring from his mouth. Behind him other noises poured up the stairs—the clang of steel, furniture crashing over, Tralthos shouting, "Treason! To the King!" at the top of his lungs. Blade grabbed for his sword, remembered as he encountered an empty scabbard that Tralthos had disarmed him, cursed, and charged down the stairs.

As he came down the stairs at a dead run he met four men with drawn swords charging upward at a pace only slightly slower than his own. Before he could ask who they were, two of them answered the question for him with wild lunges at his chest. They were too excited and hasty to aim properly. He flung himself aside, pivoting on one leg as he bounced off the wall and kicking out in a savage stroke with the other foot. It caught one of the swordsmen off balance, hurling him down the stairs to land with a scream and a thud. Blade chopped the next man across the side of the neck with the edge of his hand, plucked his sword out of the air as the man's hand went limp and released it, then engaged the other two. They were better swordsmen than their comrades, but far from good enough to match Blade. In a matter of seconds he met one with a stop-thrust, kicked his legs out from under him, thrust the other through the chest while his swing was blocked by his toppling comrade, then slashed down at the fallen man, lopping his head off as neatly as a bunch of grapes. Without waiting to check whether all four were dead, Blade snatched a dagger from the belt of the headless corpse and bounded down the blood-slick stairs.

He arrived perhaps five seconds after a sweating, swearing gang of nearly a dozen men had backed Tralthos into the entrance to the stairs, where for a moment they could only come at him one or two at a time. Some of the men wore plain tunics whose borders and rich sheen yet indicated high rank; some wore the leather and wool of hired bravos, one the uniform of a Guardsman. Behind them in the chamber Tralthos' three companions, the countess' other two guards, and half a dozen more assassins sprawled silent or groaning amid a litter of dropped weapons, smashed furniture, and bloodstained carpeting.

Blade stormed down the stairs and crashed past Tralthos into the ranks of the assassins with the force of an avalanche. They gave way. In sheer terror at the gigantic bloodspattered figure, eyes incandescent with fury, two of them turned and ran headlong down the corridor, pursued by curses from some of their comrades. Others silently turned to face Blade, wasting none of the breath needed for fighting.

Odds of ten to one (or ten to two, counting Tralthos) were long but not impossible, since Blade knew himself to be stronger and three times angrier than any of his opponents. He beat down his first opponent's guard by sheer force and thrust him through the throat, then picked up a second opponent as easily as he would have picked up a wine bottle and hurled him onto the sword point of a third. Two more came at him together. He blocked, backed away into the stair opening, and smashed one man's weapon down so that he was unguarded long enough for Tralthos to run him through the body.

There was a moment's pause as the surviving assassins backed away into the center of the wrecked chamber and stared at the two opponents standing in the doorway—standing between them and the King. Blade was not relieved by this pause. The men were desperate, their lives already forfeit, and if it occurred to them to plough through by sheer weight of numbers the seven survivors might break through the two. Then it would be up to Larina's dying guardsman and King Pelthros himself. Blade hoped the King knew how to use that sword he had put on.

Blade saw two of the men look at the others and point to a wrecked table, saw four others go over and pick it up, raising it on end to act as a shield. A human battering ram with the table as its striking end! Blade looked at

130

Tralthos and grimaced. They would have to back up the stairs. If they stayed put, they would be smashed and stunned by the coming charge.

It seemed to Blade that all the sights and sounds in the room were coming to his senses with incredible clarity—the hacked-off hand still clutching a wine cup flattened by a boot heel, the long splintery sword scar across the polished top of the table facing them, the heavy breathing of the men lifting it to the vertical. Then suddenly a gurgling scream floated down the corridor. The assassins whirled around to look behind them, dropping the table with a crash—and Blade and Tralthos charged out of the doorway.

Blade vaulted over the table into the midst of the enemy, scattering them, knocking one man clear off his feet so that Tralthos could run him through a split second later. Then he was whirling around, both sword and dagger weaving a deadly pattern, and the assassins were no longer trying to stand and fight, but scattering. Blade sprang aside from one frantic lunge, tripped over a body and went down. His emboldened opponent thrust again, missing Blade's shoulder but laying open his tunic. Blade dropped his own sword, rolled over like a log straight into the man, took his legs out from under him. Before the man could rise, Blade snatched up the leg of a chair and laid it across the back of his head. The man went limp.

Blade was conscious of Tralthos skewering one more man with contempt in every line of his thrust. Then there was a tremendous uproar in the corridor, with flaring torches and thundering boots and screams as the last of the assassins went down before a charge of the Royal Guard, a whole company coming down the corridor at a dead run. Tralthos had to stand over Blade waving the Guardsmen away, or they would have laid into him also.

Blade rose and took Tralthos' hand. The captain had redeemed himself twenty times over for the little moments of pettifoggery, with four assassins at least to his personal credit. The captain grinned, then quickly knelt down as King Pelthros appeared in the doorway, sword in hand, followed by the countess.

131

Not much to Blade's surprise, the lady found words for the occasion. "Your Majesty, look at this chamber. It is filled with the bodies of men who were coming to kill you—and of faithful servants who died in your defense. Now say if my reports of plots are imagination only!"

Pelthros, less nimble with his tongue, was silent for a considerable time. Then he said slowly, "It seems that some of it at least was the truth. I think it is time that I spoke to the Chancellor."

"If you can find him, Your Majesty. He may well be fled to the camp of the Ninth Brigade, which he intended to lead into the city once you were dead or captive."

"A whole Brigade of my army in Indhios' pay?" The King looked appalled. "This is beyond reason!"

"Perhaps beyond reason, Your Majesty," said the countess, "but not beyond Indhios' deviousness and treason."

"Yes, yes, I understand, I think. Now, my Lady, let me retire to my chambers and peruse these documents you have offered me. After that I will send for Indhios and ask him to explain his doings of late."

One does not, with impunity, lose one's temper and berate a King like an erring schoolboy, but Blade felt himself on the edge of doing so. From Larina's expression he judged that she did not feel differently. But they could only bite their tongues and shrug their shoulders as the King disappeared up the stairs and shut the door firmly behind him.

Tralthos looked at Blade. "Gods above deliver us from our King's lust for justice above everything else," he groaned. "While he sits like a clerk in his chambers, Indhios may even now—"

"Of course," said Blade. "But we need not join the King in sitting idly. Captain, could you take a few of these men and go to Indhios' apartments? He will not be there, but there may be some of his henchmen to be found who can be made to talk."

Blade saw from the expressions on the Guardsmen's faces that he had struck the proper note and responded to a widespread desire for action. None of the Guardsmen shared Pelthros' scruples about going straight into action

132

against whoever was responsible for the heaped corpses lying about this very chamber. Tralthos picked out a dozen of the toughest-looking soldiers and led them off at a noisy trot, while Blade mapped out his strategy and snapped out his orders.

Actually they were only urgings rather than orders, for he had no more legal authority to command the Guard than he had possessed an hour before. But he had the far more effective authority of a man who sees what needs to be done and has already risked his life doing some of it. His words were obeyed as readily as if they came from the King or the Commander of the Guard, and squads and sections marched away in all directions.

Some went as messengers to alert the rest of the Guard—all twenty-two companies—plus the three Brigades of the army barracked in and around High Royth, the city constabulary, and the Wardens of the Port who helped patrol the dockyards. (Blade hoped Brora had properly dealt with any trouble there but could not be sure.) Some went to patrol the corridors of the palace and keep the innocent from roaming about and the guilty from escaping by shooing everybody impartially back into their chambers. (Blade hoped the soldiers would not be too quick with their swords.) Some went to reinforce the guards on the walls to make absolutely sure that Indhios could send no one into the palace for a second attempt at storming the royal apartments. And some remained with Blade, clearing away the bodies and wreckage as much as possible, with eyes flickering constantly down the corridor in case it spewed out more surprises.

Except for Blade's orders, affairs hung in their royally decreed state of suspended animation until well after dawn. It was then that Pelthros came down from his chambers, even more red-eyed than before, with the crumpled papers under his arm, and took the countess by the hand. "My Lady, you have done the Realm and Our House a great service." He had recovered his wits enough to have reverted to the royal "we," and Blade felt it appropriate to bow.

"And you too, Champion Blahyd. Never in the four

133

centuries there have been Champions for the Kings of Royth has a Champion so well earned his name." He swept his arm around the chamber in a gesture as theatrical as anything the countess had ever used. He was obviously about to launch into another fulsome sentence when an officer of the Guard appeared, leading a party of a dozen men dressed like sailors and carrying two large brass-bound sea chests.

"From the dockyard, Your Majesty. They say—"

"Ay-y-y, Blahyd!" shouted a familiar voice from among the sailors, and Brora dashed forward and grabbed Blade by the shoulders. "I see ye've had a rare good night, aye?"

"Yes, we have."

"As 'twas w' us," said Brora with a grin. "Your Majesty, there were some traitors among your officers i' the dockyard. Here they be." He motioned the men behind him to set the chests on the floor, then strode over to them and flung open both lids.

The King gasped, the countess gave a little scream and reeled against him; even Blade found his stomach churning. Each chest held a dozen human heads, neatly or not so neatly severed, lying on blood-drenched sailcloth. It was quite a long time before anybody recovered his voice enough to thank Brora, who stood beaming at them over his handiwork. Remembering Festival and Cayla's hobbies, Blade could not find it in him to become too indignant over Brora's methods.

"Well, Brora Lanthal's son," said Pelthros finally, then paused again. "You are a—a—*thorough* man, indeed." He was apparently trying to find some way of phrasing a compliment, when the countess as usual stepped in (although Blade noticed she kept her eyes averted from the heads).

"A good spectacle indeed, Your Majesty," she said. "And perhaps some day soon we shall see all your enemies both here and abroad in a similar state. That would be an even better spectacle."

One of these days, thought Blade, Larina was going to overreach herself in seeking for dramatic comments to make at key moments, offend the King, and see all her hopes go up in smoke. Meanwhile, however, she provided a certain amount of entertainment in a situation that promised little besides a long, grim struggle.

CHAPTER 17

With the King resolved to move against Indhios, it became possible to send orders instead of merely advice to all the people Blade had previously alerted. Pelthros, to his credit, did not resent Blade's having jumped the gun. In fact, when he heard what Blade had done, he delivered several fulsome sentences declaring Blade's wits to be as sound as his arm and appointed him a High Constable of Royth.

This made Blade the equivalent of a general and made it possible for him to go right on giving orders, which he did. Fortunately, most of the people to whom he gave them did not resent his sudden promotion. They respected him, even though they might have second thoughts about King Pelthros.

Putting three Brigades plus the Royal Guard on the alert meant twenty thousand regular soldiers available for whatever was needed. This, Pelthros decided, included cordoning off the whole city and conducting a house-by-house search for weapons. Inevitably, this meant confiscating an immense quantity of swords, cutlasses, daggers, pikes, and rusty armor from thousands of peaceable citizens. This in turn led to incidents, some of them fatal to one or both sides. And of course, riots then broke out, and by nightfall a good part of the soldiers were patrolling the streets, keeping High Royth calm, rather than marching out of the city toward the camp of the Ninth Brigade.

Blade was not entirely surprised that the King's zeal for action outstripped his judgment about what action should be taken, but he was entirely unhappy about it. As the sunset turned the range of hills beyond the city purple, and the smoke spiraling up from burning houses in the waterfront district obscured the seascape, Blade sat with Larina on a high balcony of the palace and toyed with his gold cup and silver tableware. An ample meal—roast chicken stuffed with chestnuts and raisins, venison pastries, fresh bread, fruit, and bottles of wine—covered a black marble table between them. Blade had not eaten anything substantial since the night before and should have been demolishing the meal at a great rate. But the uncertainty that still dominated the situation was knotting his stomach and making it impossible for him to eat and barely possible for him to sit still.

Finally, he could sit no longer; he drained his wine cup and stood up. "King Pelthros has done one wise thing so far in this crisis. He has made me a High Constable." His voice was bitter, so bitter that Larina neither smiled nor threw back a witty remark. "I am going to take advantage of that." He began to stride back and forth, even less able to remain motionless now that he was planning, talking in a low voice.

"The key to the whole situation is still Indhios. The conspiracy will live until we take off its head by taking off his. And the most likely place for Indhios is the camp of the Ninth Brigade. That camp hasn't been taken. It hasn't been attacked. It hasn't been besieged or even properly patrolled! The local troops and the Guard are all too busy fighting some poor wretch of a shopkeeper over his grandfather's halberd! We don't even know that the Ninth Brigade isn't marching on High Royth at this very moment! If it is, there's nothing to stop it but a few cavalry patrols. And once it's through the gates and over the walls, the citizens that Pelthros' damned foolish orders have alienated will join it, and we'll finally have the popular uprising we couldn't have had otherwise!" He was so furious at Pelthros' obstinate folly that he let his voice rise almost to a shout.

With an effort he controlled himself. "A small force of picked men, disguised and heavily armed, might be able to make it into the camp and kill or capture Indhios. After that, I doubt if the Brigade's officers will move on their own. They'll probably try to make terms. If Pelthros has any sense, he'll at least cashier them all."

Larina smiled knowingly. "And you will be leading this small force? I might have guessed it."

Blade shrugged. "As I said, I'm a High Constable of Royth. I should be able to find arms and horses for fifty men without anybody asking stupid questions. Could you call two of your guards, Larina? I would like to send messages to Captain Tralthos and Brora."

No matter how many orders a general gives, it still takes a certain amount of time to pick fifty good fighting men, equip them, and brief them for a complex and dangerous mission where any one of fifty things could go disastrously wrong. Although Blade did his best, he could not be in six places at once. It was nearly midnight before he led his force out of High Royth. They passed out through the West Gate, the same one he had passed through from the other direction as a chained prisoner only a few months before, and moved out on the Royal South Road at a canter.

When they were safely clear of the rich men's villas and scattered farms that clung to the fringes of the city, they turned sharply back to the west. Although the road narrowed almost to a trail, they kept on without slackening their speed. The raid was a desperate project at best; it would be simple suicide in daylight. By the road they were using, the camp was no more than three hours' ride west of High Royth, which should with luck give them two full hours of darkness for their work.

Blade's estimate was close enough. The chimes in the camp's shrine to Myonra, the war god, were chiming the third hour as they stopped their horses just in sight of the camp but beyond the ranges of its sentries. The turncoat soldiers were apparently concentrating entirely on defending their camp and not bothering to send out patrols, even foot ones, to cover the surrounding roads. This was a mistake, and Blade intended to take full advantage of it.

The light of the moon and the torches in the camp made it fully visible. It was a rectangle two hundred yards by three hundred, with rammed-earth walls eight feet high surmounted by a row of wooden palisades rising another five feet and sliced through all along their length by arrow slits. Inside, the tents were arrayed in smaller rectangles, each company with its own defined space, and in the center bulked the larger, permanent buildings. A whitewashed shrine, a red-painted hospital, the black squat arsenal and forge, with clangings and smoke floating up from inside it, the green-painted storehouses. In the very center was a small, square building whose gilded ornamentation blazed in the light reflected from numerous torches burning inside it and also those carried by the cordon of sentries around it. That cordon of sentries meant only one thing to Blade—someone or something important was inside that building. And there could be only one person that important in the camp—Indhios. He turned to Brora and grinned savagely.

"Ready."

Brora nodded and pulled out a black hood and a length of rope. In a few moments Blade and Tralthos were hooded and bound with knots that would instantly slip apart the moment they exerted a little force. Then one of Brora's own men bound and hooded him, one of Tralthos' sergeants took the lead, and the whole cavalcade clattered down the hill, making as much noise as possible with hoofbeats and jangling equipment and whoops of joy.

Inside the hood, Blade could only judge their progress from the sounds that came to his ears. He heard the sentries challenge and an explosion of trumpet calls as the guard was called out, and the sergeant's voice replying gleefully:

"We have some prisoners that Indhios might be interested in seeing."

There was a moment's silence. Blade found himself holding his breath.

"The count is asleep," replied the guard cautiously. Blade now found himself having to fight to keep from triumphantly shouting a war cry.

"I don't think he'll mind being awakened for these three," said the sergeant with a laugh. "Remove the masks."

138

Blade found himself in the middle of a sea of half-dressed soldiers holding torches and lanterns, all staring at him and the other "prisoners" as if they were some prodigious monsters. He tried to look fearful and uncertain. He hoped his expression didn't show the red blood lust that was filling him at the anticipation of finally coming to grips with Indhios.

The guard commander returned. "The count will see you with the prisoners. Your men can dismount and stable their horses with us."

Blade waited to see if the sergeant would come through with the cover story prepared as an answer to just that question. "Thank you, but no. We have our own base some miles from here, and our own women and wine waiting there. But you will be welcome to our hospitality there soon. The disturbances in Royth will be making many a wealthy man pack up and head for the country, and the pickings should be rich." The sergeant had the expression of a man almost licking his lips in anticipation of plunder.

"Very well. Come with me." They followed the guard through the gate of the camp. Half a dozen of the troop stayed with the three "prisoners," leading their horses at a walk up the main street of the camp, while the rest milled around by the gate. They approached the gilt-encrusted building, its torches seeming even brighter at close range. The sentries drew back to let the horsemen ride up to the door, then turned and snapped to attention as Indhios came out.

He wore a plum-colored robe with black fur trim and a gold chain around his neck, none of the rich attire doing anything to diminish his grossness. The fat hands that came up in a gesture of childish delight at the sight of Blade were covered with rings that winked in the light.

"Ah, the pirate Blahyd. This meeting will be most interesting, though I fear profitable only for myself. I shall have to tell Alixa that you are here. I am sure the poor creature will want to see you, although whether you will find much pleasure in seeing her, as she is now . . ."

There being no good reason for further delay and no

139

hope of controlling himself much longer, Blade moved. His wrists flew apart, jerking the ropes clear, and he vaulted out of the saddle straight onto Indhios. The Chancellor weighed more than Blade, but he crashed to the ground under the attack. Before the Chancellor could regain his breath or draw any of his weapons, Blade grabbed the greasy beard and hair and hammered the massive skull hard against the ground until the man stopped struggling.

Now the sentries reacted, swarming in toward the men on the ground, and found the mounted men spurring their mounts forward and bringing their swords out, to form a wall of horses and flashing steel around Blade and his prisoner. Tralthos slashed the astounded guard commander out of his saddle, jumped to the ground, and helped Blade heave the massive form of the Chancellor over the vacant saddle and tie him in place.

By this time the other soldiers in the camp were joining in the circle forming around the horsemen. They were just in time to be hit in the rear by a massed charge of the rest of the raiders. Every man in the force except for half a dozen holding the gate came riding in, swords swinging, to scatter the soldiers in all directions or drive them forward onto the equally busy swords of the men around Blade.

But they could not leave just yet. Blade laid about him furiously for a few moments, cutting a swathe in the men driven back toward him, then grabbed the count by the beard and thrust a torch toward his face. The piggish eyes opened.

"Where is Alixa?"

"I—" The count winced and closed his eyes against the glare and the heat.

"Where?"

"The—the back room. You—"

But Blade had already dashed the torch to the ground and charged into the house, chopping down one soldier who tried to bar his way so much by reflex that he hardly noticed the man falling and writhing on the floor. He spotted a door leading to what must be the back, tested it, found it locked. He stepped back a pace, seized the count's chair, a massive thing suitable for a massive man, and hurled it like a catapult stone against the door. Lock and hinges both screeched apart and the door fell with a crash.

Alixa stumbled out. Her eyes were blank and staring, her hair tangled and hanging down her back, and she wore only a greasy and blood-specked white shift. She was not a small woman, but Blade scooped her up under one massive arm as though she were a child and left the building at a run. He flung her over his horse as easily as he would a basket of fruit, vaulted into the saddle, and pulled her against him as he bellowed:

"All right, everybody. Time to move out!"

A few hardy souls tried to form an infantry line across the main street of the camp, but the full weight of the fifty charging horsemen swept over them and left them lying motionless or writhing on the trampled and bloodsmeared earth. The troop charged out into the darkness, swung left to get onto the Royal West Road, and settled down to put as much distance between them and the camp as possible in as short a time as possible.

Whether because they were too stunned or simply because they had no cavalry to spare, the Ninth Brigade did not pursue the raiders. The first sign of military activity Blade and his men met, in fact, was just after dawn when they rode back into the suburbs of High Royth and met a troop of the Guard Cavalry. The captain of the troop was a trifle skeptical of Blade's story until he saw who was riding trussed like a slaughtered deer across the back of a horse in the middle of the band following Blade. After that, he grinned broadly and waved them on. Blade rode into the city with a great confidence in the good sense of the soldiers of Royth, whatever he might think of their King.

They had to interrupt Pelthros at breakfast to present Indhios, a breakfast he was eating with the countess on the very balcony where she and Blade had dined the evening before. Pelthros, Blade noticed, looked clear-eyed now, and he was wearing a mail coat and a rather more efficient-looking sword than his former ceremonial

141

weapon. He rose as they approached, laid down knife and fork, and stepped forward a pace to glare at Indhios.

"Well, Chancellor. If you are responsible for what has happened these past two days, there is a heavy burden on you. And there will be a heavy punishment, if you are indeed guilty."

Blade once again wanted to take Pelthros by his beard the way he had taken Indhios and bang the King's head against something hard in the hope of knocking some sense into it. Wouldn't the King ever come to a decision about this traitor who had all but ruined Royth?

"You can punish me if you want to," growled Indhios. "But it won't do you any good. You won't outlive me by much, you artistic fool! And that bitch-whore beside you—" Before anyone could react, he swung one clublike arm into the stomach of the guard on his right, snatched the man's sword with the other hand, and charged straight at the King. Pelthros jumped one way, the countess jumped the other—not fast enough. The sword drove through her just below the right breast and came out her back. Letting go of the sword, Indhios turned to face them.

"You'll be damned lucky to die this easy," he growled, turned back to the railing, and with one heave of his arms pulled himself up and over. Blade snapped from his paralysis in time to see Indhios land on the stone a hundred feet below. He didn't bounce. Soldiers were already clustering around the body when Blade turned back to the countess.

"Larina, I was a fool to—"

"He—was a desperate man. I—should have—told—you—he might do—this. Don't blame—yourself." Her hand clutched at his, and she died.

Blade was conscious of Pelthros bending over his shoulder, looking down at the small, still body. There were tears in his eyes. "She shall be buried among the Queens of Royth. She did as much as any of them." He rose and looked out over his capital. "And we have much to do, to complete the work that she—and you—began."

142

CHAPTER 18

Whatever had kept Pelthros from hurling himself and his Kingdom unrestrainedly into action, the death of Indhios and the countess seemed to remove it. Pelthros was at his desk or in council for forty hours out of the next forty-eight. At the end of that time, much of what could be done to prepare the Kingdom of Royth for the attack of the pirates had been done.

The army was mobilized and the coastal garrisons reinforced. The navy was to be fully manned and most of its strength concentrated at High Royth, except for the ships out on patrol. The Wardens of the Port were alert for any efforts at sabotage, and patrolled so industriously that no small number of innocent people ended up sharing prison cells with those already arrested during the arms confiscation riots. These riots themselves faded out within a few hours after reports of the true situation were passed around. Most of the citizens of High Royth had not much use for their King but even less for the Neraler pirates.

The dockyards and arsenals were set to work on building new ships and weapons, refurbishing those in storage, and issuing full equipment to those ships and soldiers already serving. The Ninth Brigade was stripped of its standards, most of its officers cashiered, and the enlisted men parceled out into reinforcements assigned to garrisons on the western frontier of the Kingdom, a month's march from the coast. All the coastal villages were given small garrisons and all the coastal roads patrolled by cavalry.

And there were minor details, such as burying Indhios in a pauper's grave, making arrangements for a state fueral for the countess, and honoring Blade, Tralthos, and Brora. Tralthos was knighted and given command of a Guards battalion, Brora raised to the rank of captain and given a warship, and Blade further honored with the award of most of Indhios' estates. It was only when he sat

143

down and forced his mind into old memories that he re-called there was another Blade, who would someday soon (but hopefully not too soon) be called Home, and leave behind all these splendid estates—as well as Alixa.

Alixa had indeed been heavily drugged and kept drugged all during her "protective confinement" in Indhios' hands. But that was all. Even the drugs wore off within twenty-four hours, leaving her sick, shaken, weak as a kit-ten, but alive and ready to regain her strength with proper care. Pelthros saw to the proper care personally. Within a week Blade and Alixa could look out at the palace and the lights burning late from their bed.

Blade, however, found himself with little time for Alixa. He was, for better or worse, one of King Pelthros' generals, and he felt it was high time he started earning his pay. The latest reports to come in (admittedly several weeks out of date, but perhaps the more ominous for that very reason) suggested that the pirates had accumulated nearly four hundred ships at Neral. Half of these at least would be their own war galleys, half hired merchantmen and sailing warships. With such an armada they would have no trouble transporting every one of their fifty thou-sand fighters and even the ten thousand mercenaries that one horrid rumor reported. By now, the great harbor at Neral must contain so many ships that one could cross it dry shod by leaping from deck to deck.

No one was seriously suggesting that the fleet of Royth should sally out against the island. That would be like asking a flea to put out a furnace by jumping into it, and even the retired generals and admirals whose wine-soaked brains could think of nothing but "the honor of Royth" admitted that much. Without allies, the royal navy could muster perhaps a hundred and twenty warships and sev-enty to ninety supporting vessels, barely enough to give it some hope of fighting a defensive battle. And they *would* be without allies. Even if there had been time to negotiate and sign an alliance, the other three Kingdoms had been openly contemptuous of Royth's declining maritime power for years and were now openly skeptical of its chances of meeting the pirate attack. Royth was going to stand alone.

On land, though, the situation of the Kingdom was far better and gave Blade much food for thought. The royal army of Royth would number eighty thousand men when fully mobilized, and there were also fifty thousand more in local militia units, police forces, customs guards, the Wardens of the Port, and the like—perhaps untrained but not unenthusiastic. Considering the pirates' lack of experience in large-scale land warfare, it should in theory be easy to meet and defeat them once they got ashore.

The problem was that these troops had to defend two thousand miles of land frontiers as well as six hundred miles of coast, at least half of that coast suitable for the landing of the pirate host. Scattered thus, it would be a miracle if the royal army could mass more than fifteen thousand men in any one place without leaving undefended some place that needed defense. And even assembling that many would take several days, during which time the pirates could put their whole force ashore anywhere along the usable coastline and march inland, ravaging the countryside wherever they went. When the royal army came down on them, they would have plenty of warning and plenty of time to force it to meet them on ground and at a time of their own choosing. Under such circumstances, experience or no experience, the pirates might well win a devastating victory, breaking King Pelthros' army and the morale of his subjects.

But there was an idea glimmering in Blade's mind all through one sleepless night. In the morning he rose, sat down at his desk and wrote it up in a form fit for presentation to the War Council.

The pirates would never send their full strength ashore until they had met and defeated the royal fleet. Suppose that they were led to believe that the royal fleet was as good as defeated even before they appeared on the coast? They would hardly be able to turn down such an opportunity for an easy victory. They would most probably make straight for the nearest spot of coast, anchor their ships, and set to plundering. Blade knew the pirates' lack of discipline when it came to easy loot; they would scatter all over the countryside in a matter of days, out of all control

145

by their captains. That was the great reason why the pirates had never managed a full-scale invasion before, even more than their lack of prowess at land fighting.

And suppose the pirates could be induced to land and then scatter their forces in a stretch of country within easy striking distance of a large force of royal troops? Springing out of concealment, thirty thousand royal troops could sweep up the pirate detachments one by one. Even if the royal fleet could not then move out and take the undermanned and immobilized pirate fleet in the rear, the blow to the pirates' strength in manpower would be devastating.

Blade realized that without many details which he did not yet have the local knowledge to supply, the whole plan had an armchair-general flavor that made him pause and would certainly make others object. But those others might also be able to fill in the details. It would certainly start people thinking about ways to get out of the dilemma caused by the pirates' ability to strike whenever they wished with their whole force. That dilemma was paralyzing the ability of the War Council to plan. Blade realized that Royth was not weak, nor were its leaders, when all was said and done. But they had a problem—a flaw that might be about to become fatal—in their inability to see the strengths they possessed.

So he drew up his plan in as much detail as he could and presented it that evening to the War Council. "Fantastic" was the mildest word he heard used about it, and if the situation had been less desperate, Blade had no doubt that Pelthros himself would have come down hard on the side of his older and allegedly wiser military leaders and refused even to permit a debate. But the situation was desperate, the debate took place, and in it some of the younger officers who had held their peace while their seniors fulminated spoke up for Blade.

"There *is* a river in Northcoast Province where we could hide the fleet secure from discovery," said a young squadron commander. "It's called the Keltz, and the country around it is so wooded and sparsely populated that we could hide ten fleets and three armies there until they died

146

of old age. And we could make it possible for the fleet to get out again in a hurry, too. There's only one usable passage through the sandbars at the mouth of the river now, but we could dredge out several more in a week's work. It's never been done before because there aren't enough people up there to make it worthwhile."

"Very good," said Blade. "If the pirates have charts of the coast, they will be certain that our fleet could only get out one or two ships at a time. They will probably leave no more than a small squadron on patrol. And so our fleet can pour out and catch the pirates in the rear, and perhaps by surprise."

That idea made even the most crusted old men sit up and grin gleefully. But the objections were now joined by Pelthros himself. "We see much wisdom in your plan, Constable Blahyd," he said. "But to draw the pirates inland, we must needs leave a large expanse of our territory and many of our subjects exposed to barbarities which you yourself know well. What say you to that?"

"I say that if we arrange it so the pirates land close to where we have both the army and the fleet, we can strike at them quickly and reduce the damage they do. But I beg you to consider accepting the risk even of great damage. If this plan works, the pirate power will be broken for all time, and next year Your Majesty can even consider leading forth your forces against Neral itself! The name of Royth will shine forever with a mighty glory for having smitten the pirates down into the sea!" Blade wondered if he was developing a weakness of his own for melodramatic statements on all possible and impossible occasions.

"True enough," said the King. "But if we understand you, what you wish is that both the army and the navy be massed well to the north. What assurance can we have that the pirates will land where we wish, and not make straight for High Royth? The city would be left almost defenseless by your plan."

"I beg to differ, Your Majesty. High Royth is a mighty city, the jewel of your realm, and heavily fortified. It can stand alone against the pirates for many weeks, certainly long enough for your army to assemble and crush the pirates if they are massed around its walls. It can fall swiftly only through treachery, which Your Majesty's vigilance has rendered impossible." After your procrastination nearly rendered it successful, he would have liked to have added, but politeness to kings usually pays dividends. "And if your loyal subjects can be given back their arms and told to hold them ready for use against the pirates, I am sure you can leave High Royth with even fewer soldiers than usual."

The King contemplated that for a moment, then said, "Likewise true. Or true enough to deserve our consideration. But it would still be an ill thing for our capital to be besieged by the Neralers. Have you a scheme for indeed leading them to some place under the noses of our fighting men?"

Blade swallowed. The War Council had been purged of the treasonous, he hoped, but had it been purged of the garrulous? He—or the half-forgotten Richard Blade of Home Dimension, actually—had seen too many cover stories or ruses blown to smithereens because some fool knew too much and then had one drink too many. But he was in too deep to back out.

"I do. Let the rumor be circulated that the Kingdom's gold and other valuables from both public and private sources are being moved—for safety—to some place in this area." He tapped the map in the general area of the northeast corner of the Kingdom. "The thought of carrying away the whole royal treasury of Royth at a single blow will be enough to make the pirates search every hayloft and under every rock for it. And if we also fortify a number of towns and villages in the area, we can provide refuges for the country people and also delay the advance of the pirates until the royal army is ready to strike."

Pelthros nodded, with a look on his face of a man becoming largely but not yet entirely convinced.

"We would prefer to see some reliable way of getting word of the bait to the pirates. If Indhios had not been killed and his faction smashed, we could have dropped hints where he would pick them up and convey them to

148

his allies. Perhaps we could present the rumor as coming from him still?" He appeared to be asking Blade.

Blade shook his head. "I fear not, Your Majesty. Had we smashed Indhios' faction less publicly, we could expect the pirates not to know that it had gone. But I am sure that boats are already bound for Neral, carrying the word. Indhios not only fell from power, he fell from a great height before a thousand witnesses. Anything that was supposed to come from Indhios, the pirates would know to be a trap."

Before Pelthros could say anything in reply, Blade went on. "I think the best way for passing word of the bait might be for me to take a small ship, manned by my own men, and sail out to meet the pirates as though I were joining them. Or rejoining them," he added with a wry grin.

There were murmurs and rumbles of surprise all around the Council table, from younger and older members alike. Pelthros was the first to put his thoughts into words, and shocked enough to let the royal "we" slip.

"I appreciate your—your idea. But—won't they simply kill you outright before you can speak to them?"

Blade shook his head. "I know the Truce Code of the Brotherhood, which is inviolate. Even a man forsworn from the Brotherhood or outlawed from it can invoke Truce for twenty-four hours once in his life. I admit, some hothead may still put an arrow through me. But I could be supplied with maps and documents that will get the word to the pirates even if I die. And of course, if they kill me after I have spoken to them, my job will have been done."

If Blade had, like the late countess, been striving for dramatic effects, he would have been amply rewarded by the spectacle of twenty of the highest statesmen and soldiers in Royth reduced to an amazed silence. And when he saw Pelthros nod slowly, and go on nodding until looks of approval appeared on the faces all around the table, he knew that he had won. He would enjoy honor and influence in Royth second only to Pelthros himself, for his idea had impressed the younger leaders and his grand gesture

149

in laying his own life on the line had impressed the older ones. Whether he would ever live to enjoy that honor and influence was, of course, another matter.

CHAPTER 19

Blade watched the horizon grow sawtoothed with the sails of the pirate fleet. He suddenly realized that at last he was as calm as he had pretended to be since the War Council three weeks ago.

He had been on edge with the strain of waiting all during those weeks, a strain which not even the frantic bouts of lovemaking with Alixa could relieve. The strain was made worse by the fact that he himself had little to do with the preparations for trapping the pirates. His moment would come only when the fleet was reported in sight, and Pelthros insisted that in the meantime he and his crew (actually, Brora's crew) have a chance to rest, gain strength, and indulge themselves. There was a certain note of "the hearty last meal for the condemned man" in Pelthros' well-intentioned decision that made Blade feel no better.

So he watched from the windows of his luxurious suite in the palace, with Alixa beside him, as the royal fleet sailed north, a hundred warships and a hundred merchant vessels carrying extra soldiers, supplies, and the labor gangs who would dredge out the mouths of the Keltz. By night, he heard the rumble of wheels, the tramp of soldiers, and the harsh voices of sergeants calling cadence as the Royal Guard and a brigade from the garrison of High Royth moved out, northward bound also, to join the army assembling there. In the early morning as he walked through the marketplaces and arcades, unable to sleep or even lie still beside the sleeping Alixa, he saw men polishing pikes and halberds, piling stones and firewood, weaving ropes for catapults. And then he would go home, to sit detached and distant over a breakfast prepared by the

King's own cooks, replying to Alixa's questions only with grunts or mutters until she sometimes burst into tears.

Then finally word came from a merchant vessel that ran herself frantically on the rocks at the mouth of the harbor in her flight. The pirates were in sight and no more than a day's sail off the coast. That night, Blade had no trouble talking to Alixa, nor she to him, as they writhed and tossed in a wild passionate agony and then lay feeble as children in the tangled sheets.

Blade was up long before dawn the next morning, riding alone through the dark and dew-slick streets to the pier where Brora was putting the final touches on their ship, a light galley named *Charger*. Brora threw Blade a salute as he rode up, then grinned and said, "Aye, I'm becomin' too much the naval officer to remember how to be a pirate!"

"You'll be a better naval officer for having been a pirate, I think," said Blade. "We can all learn something from a man like Tuabir."

"Aye," said Brora. "May Druk keep him an' be merciful. Perhaps we'll be findin' out about Druk's mercy ourselves before the day be o'er."

Blade grinned. "Don't give up the ship until she sinks under you." He sprang down from the saddle and strode up the gangplank, calling greetings to the men he recognized. That was most of them, for all but a handful of *Charger's* forty-odd men had been part of *Thunderbolt's* crew or at least of Brora's action squads in the dockyard.

Half an hour later, with her blue and white sails to a rising dawn breeze and the sky behind her beginning to pale, *Charger* slipped past the breakwater and plunged out to sea. She was out of sight of land by mid-morning, and the cook had just called the hands to lunch when the foremast lookout squalled his warning. Blade ran forward, and a few minutes later he could see it too—the entire seaward horizon a forest of sails as the pirate fleet rose into view.

He suspected it would be a while before the pirates sighted *Charger*, small and low as she was. But before too long, he knew that two or three of the pirate galleys would

151

race out toward her from the long line ahead. The interesting part would begin when they recognized his personal code flags and the Truce flags flying from *Charger's* masthead. He gave the orders for the crew to pull in their oars and pull on their armor, then went below to his own cabin to equip himself. Seeing *Charger* completely defenseless might be enough to overcome some of the pirates' scruples about violating Truce.

When he returned to the deck, he saw that two galleys were in fact pulling out ahead of the pirate fleet and closing on *Charger*. Blade strained to identify them, shading his eyes from the sun—then gulped as he recognized the badges on the approaching sails. One was the late Esdros' *Spider Prince*, the other was Cayla's own *Sea Witch*. Gasps and mutterings from the crew as they crowded forward to look told him that they also had recognized the approaching ships. Of all the Captains of the Brotherhood, Cayla was the most likely to be driven by a lust for vengeance to throw caution and tradition to the winds and violate Truce. But there was nothing they could do about it without abandoning their whole plan, except what Brora was already doing—going among the men and warning them to be prepared for anything, with their weapons ready to hand.

Sea Witch was coming up so fast that even from miles away Blade could see the water foaming white at her ram and under her flashing oars. Cayla was obviously eager to come up with him and was driving her rowers along at a deadly pace. Within a few more minutes, Blade could make out every detail of *Witch*, now miles ahead of her consort—details including Cayla herself, standing on the quarterdeck as rigid as a stone statue. She did not move, nor did any of the other armed men on her ship's deck. *Witch* might have been a ship manned by statues, the oars pulling her along moved by magic.

Those oars did not stop until *Sea Witch* glided to a stop off to port of *Charger*, and her crew came pouring on deck fully armed. Cayla was also wearing armor, Blade noticed—a crested metal helm and a contoured leather cuirass that yet left her with an oddly sexless appearence.

But the voice that called across the hundred feet of water to Blade was the same as before, except for a new note of deadly rage.

"Well, Blahyd, how has being a traitor suited you?"

"What makes you think I am a traitor?" he shouted back.

That jerked her violently into silence for a moment and caused the men on *Witch's* deck to look at her and then at each other. Another moment, and she shouted back:

"You slay Indhios, slaughter his picked men like sheep, and now you come and say you have not betrayed the Brotherhood? Indhios would have given us Royth like a roast pig on a platter, and now he is dead. Dead at your hand, you traitor!" Her voice had risen to a scream, and Blade saw her crew drawing swords and nocking arrows to their bows. He motioned his own crew to do the same, then replied, making his voice sound full of injured innocence:

"Indhios was as much of a traitor to the Brotherhood as to Royth. Or at least he would have been. And the Brotherhood would have been destroyed in discovering this." Cayla's head jerked in astonishment, and Blade pressed his advantage, his voice becoming more urgent. "Indhios didn't want to rule Royth as the puppet of the Brotherhood. He wanted to rule it in his own right. He would have betrayed Royth, all right, and let you do all the hard work of destroying *his* enemies. Then he would have turned on you with his own men and destroyed you or driven you out. Then he could have ruled Royth as its savior from the pirates." Blade had a stack of carefully forged documents below in his cabin to prove his arguments. He wondered if he would need them. Such a double betrayal would have been just like Indhios, and he suspected that the wiser heads among the pirates knew that already. But the experience of the other Richard Blade, the top-ranking secret agent, was guiding him now, with memories of how important it could be to support a lie as fully as possible.

Blade couldn't read the expressions on the faces staring at him over *Witch's* railing. But the total silence on the

153

other ship's deck made him hope his words had left some sort of impression. He saw heads turning toward him, then Cayla waving one hand in a chopping gesture. *Witch's* men slipped their arrows back into the quivers and their swords back into their scabbards. Blade took a deep breath. Cayla hailed him again:

"You have invoked Truce, Blahyd. And you bring word that might best be laid before the Council of Captains. Otherwise I would take your ship and kill your men before your eyes, then send your cods to your high-born doxy! You will follow me." She turned her back decisively to bark orders to her crew, who began dropping down to the rowing benches. *Sea Witch* swept away while *Charger* turned under Brora's orders to fall in astern of her, and *Spider Prince* curved round in a great circle to take up a position at the very rear. Like a convict and two guards, the three ships set off for their goal, the ever-growing pirate fleet that now blackened fully half the horizon.

At the brutal pace *Witch* set, they came up with the advance guards of the pirate armada within half an hour. Blade saw familiar badges on the sails of the galleys as they fell behind and saw their crews pointing and staring at his own flags and the Truce banners flying from *Charger's* masts.

Beyond the advance guard lay a stretch of open sea, then the main body. Four hundred ships now seemed a conservative estimate of its total strength, Blade felt. There seemed to be an endless arc of galleys interspersed with high-prowed merchant vessels, now stretching completely across Blade's field of vision, and seeming to reach around to either side to engulf the three ships racing up to it. He could see the sun winking on helms and weapons aboard some of the merchant vessels, the intricate frames of catapults and ballistas on the high castles of others, skiffs and pinnaces with bright orange and blue and gold sails darting back and forth among the larger ships, like swallows around cliffs.

Blade soon saw that Cayla was leading them toward a particular ship, a huge merchantman even larger than Khystros' long-gone *Triumph*. From its three masts

154

streamed the green and white banner of the Captain's Council of the Brotherhood, the same that Blade had seen over Council House on Neral. As *Charger* drew closer and the flagship loomed higher and higher over him, Blade saw that her decks were crowded not only with armed soldiers, but with Captains in full battle gear, as well as their ceremonial white baldrics and green cloaks. It appeared that *Charger* had arrived in the middle of a full meeting of the Council itself. Blade wondered what the Captains had been discussing before and smiled at the havoc he would be wreaking on their carefully planned agenda. Those Captains senior enough or distinguished enough to win seats upon the Council were also often old enough to have developed a taste for complicated paperwork and tidy agendas.

The seniors were out in even greater force than usual, judging from the amount of gray and white in the beards that appeared at the railing as *Charger* ranged alongside the flagship. A rope ladder plummeted down onto *Charger's* deck. Blade caught it nimbly and scrambled up to the deck of the flagship.

As he stepped onto the deck, so did Cayla on the other side of the ship. The mercenaries and even the Captains eased themselves out of her path as she strode toward Blade. He could read her expression now—suspicion, hatred, and sheer cold fury mixed in constantly changing proportions. She too was now wearing the emblems of a Council member, a sight that made Blade even warier. She must have been rising fast and far in influence to take a seat on the Captain's Council while still barely thirty.

She stood watching him, hands clasped behind her back and feet braced apart, while the High Captain, chairman of the Council, ran through the formal greetings in a chilly and perfunctory manner. Not even for a traitor would the Brotherhood now violate a proclaimed Truce, but the control Blade saw written in many faces was stretched thin.

When the High Captain had finished speaking, the sudden silence and the eyes turned his way told Blade that it was now up to him. "Captains," he began. "I did indeed

155

flee from Neral, and it was indeed after slaying a fellow Captain. But that Captain and certain others—" he glared at Cayla, whose face showed no reaction "—for reasons of their own attempted to murder me by night in my own quarters. I defended myself, slaying Esdros and some of his companions. I plead guilty to bad judgment in having fled and suborned my crew to help me flee, rather than await the justice of the Brotherhood." He hoped that last bit of flattery would go over well with some of the senior Captains. But he could see no change in the frozen faces staring at him.

"So I came to Royth, and far from being welcomed as a traitor to the Brotherhood, was cast in prison and only liberated by unexpected influences." He would not have Larina's name dragged into this debate if he could avoid it; he owed her that much. "As I gained the freedom to move about, I saw that Indhios was planning to betray not only the Kingdom of Royth, but afterwards the Brotherhood, and rule over the ruins of both. He was a man to whom it came naturally to betray everyone in succession." That, at least, was no lie. "So I set myself to defeat him, for the good of the Brotherhood, and did so. How, I am sure you all know." There was still no thawing of the faces confronting him, but heads began to nod. The silence went on until the High Captain cleared his throat.

"Blahyd," he said shortly. "You have proof of this?"

"I do."

"Let it be brought before the Council, then." He turned sharply on one seabooted heel and strode away toward the aft cabin, the other Council members following him, all except Cayla, who glided like a prowling cat over to Blade and hissed in his ear (at least it sounded like a serpent's hissing to Blade's tight nerves), "Remember, Blade. I will denounce you if I once suspect you of telling a lie."

Blade nodded. "I still serve the Brotherhood, Cayla. Why should I tell a lie? It seems to me that *you* have more to conceal. How many of the Captains will fight to restore the rule of the Serpent Priestesses, I ask you? Denounce me, and they will find out all you so freely told me."

Cayla sprang back as though she had stepped barefoot on hot coals, and her face turned white and red and then white again with rage. Her lips tightened until they were bloodless; then she let out a long, whistling breath and nodded. Blade waited until she was out of earshot, then let his own breath out in a long sigh. He was gambling that Cayla was still so committed to her fantasies of reviving the Serpent Cult that a threat to reveal them in open Council would intimidate her. If he could keep her from stripping the "cover" off his—and Royth's—cover story, he felt he had at least a fighting chance of convincing the Brotherhood to follow the desired course.

It was indeed a "fighting" chance that the Council gave him, when they sat in the great cabin of the flagship to listen to his story in more detail. After three hours of presenting his own arguments and listening to the Council wrangle, Blade felt as wrung-out and sweat-soaked as he had felt after more than one battle.

He had spent only a few minutes of those three hours reviewing what had happened between his flight from Neral and Indhios' fall. Whether they held him innocent or not, the Council apparently had little interest in that part of his adventures. Indhios was dead; he could not be revived. "So," as one elderly Captain put it, "we need to play with the cards Blahyd dealt us, whether we will or no."

What really kept the Council's attention centered on him was his story of the panic in Royth. No part of that story was a total lie. Everything happening in Royth over the past few weeks was, he knew, known to the pirates. It was simply a question of shading the truth, of revealing the actions but hiding the motives.

The royal navy of Royth—fled northwards, its commanders crying out that they were too weak to fight the pirates, too weak to do anything but hide themselves until the pirate fleet had departed. (Savage laughter around the Council table; words such as, "By the time we've departed, they'll have naught left to defend save the bare bones of the Kingdom!") Likewise, the royal army, scattering into garrisons in a frantic effort to defend every key place

157

at once. (The pirates—and even more, the mercenary officers—didn't even bother to laugh at that. They only grinned fiercely.) High Royth in turmoil, stripped of its garrison, some citizens making desperate efforts to arm themselves, others clogging the roads inland in headlong flight, some simply cowering in their houses, hoping to escape notice when the pirates stormed over the walls. (More mocking grins.) The gold and precious stones from the royal treasury dispatched north, in a hastily assembled convoy of wagons—

"How much of the treasury?" from the mercenary commander, and the Council looking at their hired man with sourness at his intervening in the discussion.

"I'm not absolutely sure. I heard reports of at least twenty million crowns, perhaps half again that much. It was a huge convoy—two or three miles of wagons, and a whole cavalry brigade riding escort." Blade broke off and tried not to grin too openly in response to the lust for gold that he saw spreading across every face in the Council—except Cayla's.

"Mmmmmm," said one of the Captains after a long silence. He sounded like a small boy just offered a lifetime supply of ice cream.

"I think—" began another Captain, paused, then went on quickly. "I think they are practically throwing their gold into our hands. And if we take all their gold . . ." He seemed too stunned by the prospect to be able to finish his sentence.

"Yes," said the High Captain. "If we can take all of Royth's gold at a single blow, it won't matter whether or not we defeat their fleet and army this time. They will be so crippled that we can return with an even larger force next year and finish them off."

One of the oldest Captains, judging from his completely white hair and beard, began to bristle. "Are you suggesting that we hire even *more* mercenaries, bought soldiers not of the Brotherhood, rather than rely on our own strength? Where then is our victory—our honor—?"

"Where is your sense, Fenz?" snapped the High Captain. "Royth is our enemy, and it matters little how we

158

smash them if smash them we do. Does anyone care to join Fenz in disputing that?" The High Captain's hand dropped toward his sword hilt. Fenz glared at the High Captain and fingered his dagger, and Blade saw others do the same. Again, he had to fight back a grin. Sowing dissent among the Council Captains was something he had hoped for but hardly expected.

Cayla's voice sliced through the building tension like a knife cutting fruit. "Why count our gold before we have it in our hands? Blahyd, do you know *where* this mighty convoy was going?"

"Not certainly. I stole a map that shows the general area where they were going to hide the gold, but many different cities are marked on it."

"Where is that map?"

"Aboard my ship."

An immediate flurry of orders as men were sent out to bring Blade's files from *Charger* and others to bring in wine and food. Blade, in spite of his taut nerves, found he was ravenously hungry, and in politeness the Council permitted him to eat with them. Eventually—perhaps three-quarters of an hour, although seeming to Blade like three-quarters of a day—both the meal and the perusal came to an end. The High Captain handed the map, now well splotched with gravy and wine stains, back to Blade. Then he rose, placed his hands on his Baldric of Office, and addressed the Council according to the traditional formula:

"Captains of the Council of the Brotherhood. I, High Captain, say unto you: let each say yea or nay that we shall sail north in search of the horded gold of the Kingdom of Royth. And as ye hope for the blessing of Druk and honor among your Brothers and the great glory of the Brotherhood, speak only your true mind, and when all have spoken abide by the decision of the greater part." He began calling out the names of the Captains. There were twenty-five in all, and when all twenty-five had spoken out, the "decision of the greater part" stood nineteen to six in favor of going north.

Blade sagged into his chair at the release of tension. He

159

had done his part in the plan, whatever happened to him now. And Cayla seemed to have some ideas on that score, the way she was looking at him. He was not surprised when her voice again cut in.

"What are we going to do with Blahyd?"

"What do you want to do with him, Captain?" said the High Captain. A number of other Captains chuckled and still others threw out bawdy remarks that made Cayla again flare red, then turn pale and speak in a clipped voice.

"He deserted the Brotherhood, even if *you* think he did not betray it. And now he has convinced us to sail north in search of Pelthros' gold. What is there to show he will not desert us again, running off to warn Pelthros so that His Artistic Majesty can lay a trap for us?"

Blade thanked both the local and Home Dimension gods that his plan did not depend on his being free. The forces of Royth could carry out their part of it whether he was with them or not, or even whether he was alive or not. Cayla was obviously determined to do as much to him as the Council would let her do—or as much as the Council could be persuaded to overlook. And she had raised the possibility of a trap. Oh well, if she hadn't, there would have been somebody else intelligent enough to do it. The nods around the Council table indicated that much.

"Very well, Cayla," said the High Captain. "You are quite possibly right. Will you take charge of him yourself? Or do you wish another to bear the burden of carrying out your idea?"

Cayla bridled at the High Captain's tone of voice, but said nothing in reply beyond, "I will accept him."

"Good." The High Captain rose again and spoke in his formal tone. "The Council of Captains of the Brotherhood has decided. Let the orders go out: we sail north. And may Druk prosper the Brotherhood in this undertaking."

When Blade came on deck, escorted by four mercenaries with short swords and javelins, the Council's decision had already hurled the fleet into a frenzy of activity. Men were swarming up the flagship's rigging to make extra

160

sail and double-man the lookout posts. Rainbow strings of signal flags soared up the mizzenmast and were answered in kind from nearby ships. Amidships, two dozen armed guards were climbing down the rope ladder onto the deck of *Charger*. Blade saw Brora standing in their path, tension and alertness written in every line of his stance, and shouted down to him to let the guards go where they would. Farther aft, a crew of sailors under the profane urgings of a bearded bosun's mate was breaking out a thick hawser and paying it out over the side onto *Charger's* deck. Blade realized that both he and his ship would be closely guarded on the voyage north. And afterwards? He had just reached the point of speculating on that when he heard a footstep behind him and turned away from the spectacle to face Cayla.

Although they were almost breathing into each other's faces this time, he could read no expression in any of her features. She once more had herself totally under control, both body and voice.

"Well, Blahyd, you have won your victory."

"Sister Captain, the Brotherhood has won it." He could not relax one bit of his pose as a fanatically loyal Brother, least of all with this bitter, deadly, suspicious woman.

"The Brotherhood is too busy dividing the gold they have yet to see to worry about the difference. I hope—for your sake—there is none. If there is . . ." She shook her head. "If you do not betray the Brotherhood, I have no choice but to let you survive betraying *me*." Her voice dropped. "And the Sisters of the Serpent." She bared her teeth in a death's-head smile. "But if you betray the Brotherhood, there will be none to complain if I avenge both betrayals at once. And I have allies to help in my vengeance." She cocked her head to one side and directed her eyes over the side at the water, as if she could see through the shimmering surface and the green and blue fading down below into the depths. Blade would not permit his face to suggest that he knew what she was talking about, but he felt a cold chill. It was a stronger chill than the sudden shadow that fell over them both could cause, the sudden shadow of the sails as the flagship came about on her new course northwards.

CHAPTER 20

When Blade came up onto the flagship's deck after breakfast, he found the same scene that had greeted him every morning for the past week. To seaward a flat, glazed blue sea stretched to meet a glowing blue sky, the sea broken only by the sails of the patrol ships and the sky by a few puffs of white cloud.

Toward the land, the first thing he always saw was *Charger*, tied up alongside the flagship like a kitten snuggling up to its mother. Men were moving on her decks—the guards, leaning wearily against the masts and railings in postures that reeked of boredom, and her own crew, washing down the decks and airing hammocks under Brora's supervision. On either side of the flagship a line of merchant vessels stretched off for miles into the distance, their sails furled and decks bare except for morning working parties and officers taking the air like Blade. These were the deep-draft transports, which drew too much water to anchor closer in or run up on the beach.

Farther in toward the land a line of galleys and smaller merchant vessels tugged at their anchors. Beyond them still another line of masts rose into the air, marking the galleys actually drawn up on the beach. Amid those masts rose the thin curls of blue smoke marking the cooking fires of the camps on shore.

Then the land climbed into swelling green hills, marching away and blurring into the faint haze that shrouded the landward horizon. The nearest hill was surmounted by a scar of black—the ruins of a small fishing village. The ruins had been smoldering as late as two days before, long after the flames and screams that rose into the night as the pirates sacked the village had died away.

It had taken the pirates two days to sail north to their

chosen landing point and another day to put ashore their landing force, fortify the camp, and anchor or beach their ships. Cayla's fear of a trap had had some effect; the pirate fleet was less vulnerable to a seaward attack than Blade had hoped it would be. But it would most certainly be short-handed. On the fourth day the landing force had marched off into the hills, more than thirty thousand men in four great columns. Occasional faint spots of fire in the night and distant pillars of smoke by day showed where they were spreading out across the countryside in search of the gold horde of Royth. Otherwise, they might as well have all marched off the edge of the world—or into a sealed trap laid by the army of Royth. Blade hoped it was the latter.

The flagship was coming awake around him now. Smoke curled up into the almost windless air from the galley smokestack as the cooks prepared breakfast. All the fresh provisions were long gone; breakfast would probably be another unappetizing mush of pounded biscuit and minced salt meat. Amidships, the officer of the watch was looking importantly around him, taking bearings on the neighboring ships to make sure the flagship had not dragged her anchors during the night. Forward, one of the anchor windlasses creaked as a working party hauled buckets of seawater for washing the decks thirty feet straight up from the sea. One of the armorers squatted on the deck with a large pot of paint, carefully dipping the tips of catapult bolts into it.

The faint *brrrum-brrrum-brrrum* of an oarmaster's drum beating out a cruising stroke came over the water to Blade. Turning, he saw *Sea Witch* gliding past, Cayla for once sitting rather than standing by the tiller, her unhelmeted blonde head gleaming bright in the sun. She raised an arm in mocking salute as *Witch* cut across the flagship's stern, heading out to take up her patrol station. Blade was glad when the other ship passed out of his field of view. Seeing *Witch* and Cayla reminded him always of her murmured words about the allies she had, to deal with Blade in case of treachery.

Yet somehow on such a day, all stillness and color and

163

sunlight, it was hard to believe in the slithering submarine monstrosities that Blade's imagination conjured up out of his memories and his fears. He had seen no signs of them during the voyage north or the week of waiting. Perhaps they could not survive so far from the haunted waters of Mardha where they laired.

But he had also seen no signs of the royal fleet of Royth. That was much less welcome. How long would the fleet wait in its northern lair before bursting out and taking the pirates in the rear? They were less than a day's sail north of the pirate anchorage. Had Pelthros' admirals developed cold feet? The trap had to close on both the pirate fleet and the pirate army to make the victory complete. If only their army was destroyed or driven away, the whole thing might have to be done over again in a few years, regardless of what he had said in the Council. Blade found himself sweating with more than the rising heat of the sun and pacing the deck like a caged animal, until he caught himself and forced himself to sit down and at least look calm.

Breakfast arrived—what he had expected. He pulled out a wooden spoon and sat down on a canvas stool to eat. The shrieks of squabbling seabirds floated up from aft as the cooks emptied the garbage over the side.

Then all at once Blade saw smoke gush into the air at the far northern end of the line of merchant vessels. Some seconds later a dull thud floated down the line to his ears. He saw eyes swivel to follow his own gaze and took a closer look.

Oily gray-brown smoke was pouring up from a ship anchored close in the lee of the little peninsula marking the northern end of the bay. Even as Blade watched, another ship spouted smoke and this time flame, and splashes went up beside a third one. Somebody up on the peninsula was doing remarkably good shooting with a siege engine firing—what? Pots of burning oil, most likely.

Blade didn't wait to wonder who was attacking or why at this time. Only one force could be striking at the pirates here and now. Why the royal fleet was attacking its superior opponent in broad daylight was something to consider later. Right now there was not a split second to spare for either him or *Charger* if they wanted to get clear of the pirate armada safely.

He had only his eating dagger; the first thing to get was a weapon. The guard assigned to him was too busy looking north to notice anything else until he found himself jerked off his feet and over the railing by two colossal arms. Blade barely had a chance to get a good grip on his new sword when two other guards ran at him, pikes leveled. He launched a kick at one that took him down with a smashed kneecap and opened the throat of the other with a backslash. Then he dashed forward, toward the galley smokestack, snatching up the stunned armorer's paint pot on the run.

He whipped his arm up in an underarm swing, and the paint pot arched through the air like a cricket ball and dropped out of sight down the smoking galley stack. Blade was already backing away, dueling furiously with three sailors, when the galley stack spewed black smoke and orange flames. Screams floated up from below as the galley fires erupted all over the cooks. Smoke was already beginning to billow up through the hatches as Blade ran lightly up the ladder to the foc's'le, locked both arms around the windlass rope, and slid down it to the sea.

He landed near *Charger's* stern, to be almost at once nearly knocked silly by the body of a mercenary guard that came sailing over the stern railing, a cutlass firmly rammed through its chest. He swam forward to the waist, keeping on the side of *Charger* away from the flagship for safety's sake, then seized the mooring line of one of the boats bobbing there and hauled himself furiously up the side onto the deck of his own ship. It was the first time he had stood there in nearly ten days.

Another mercenary ran at him as he got to his feet. Blade, seeing that the man was trying to flee rather than trying to kill, sidestepped his clumsy lunge, tripped him, and pitched him head first over the side. It seemed now to Blade that all his trained perceptions and reflexes were operating at a higher pitch than ever before, now that the final moment of action had arrived. So it was a fighting machine that saw and heard and felt everything, and killed nearly everything in its path that sprang into combat.

One of the crew was trying to hack through the hawser holding *Charger* to the flagship. A soldier ran at him, ran him through, then died with Blade's sword jutting out through his chest. Blade whipped the sword free just in time to hack down a javelin thrust at him and take off the wielder's arm on the backswing. Another man darted past Blade, snatched up the fallen axe, swung it down on the hawser. Blade in his turn snatched up the javelin and hurled it to bring down a soldier backing a sailor against the foremast, then whirled around to face two more soldiers.

One was apparently the commander of the guards aboard *Charger*, judging from his gilded helmet and jeweled sword hilt. He was also a dangerously effective opponent. His long sword darted in and out; Blade frantically parried both the officer's lightning thrusts and the clumsier slashes of the soldier—then the hawser parted with a twang. The deck lurched slightly, throwing the officer off balance long enough for the man with the axe to whip around and bury the head in the other's back. Going down, the officer blocked his subordinate for long enough to let Blade get through the man's clumsy guard and take him in the throat. The two soldiers fell across each other, writhed briefly, then lay still in the blood sluicing across the deck.

Blade suddenly realized that the man who had chopped through the hawser and then cut down the officer was Brora, that the deck was clear of living soldiers, and that *Charger* was now nearly fifty yards clear of the flagship. He looked back toward the bigger vessel in time to see the foremast boom into a column of flame that spouted above even the black smoke pouring up from below, then turned back to Brora. The sailor was drenched with sweat and the blood oozing from half a dozen minor wounds, but grinned as he looked at Blade.

"Back to our true colors, aye, Captain Blahyd?"

"Yes. Order the men to the oars. I'm going aloft." Blade dropped his sword to the deck, grasped the ratlines, and scrambled upward toward the maintop. Once there, he at last had the view and at least a little of the time he needed to look about him and see what was happening.

The far northern end of the pirate fleet had dissolved into a chaos of burning ships and others that moved purposefully among them—galleys of all sizes, painted a green so dark that they were barely visible against the sea. The shore-based siege engines had apparently ceased fire, because of too much risk of hitting friendly ships. Farther out, off the tip of the peninsula, a mass of merchant vessels and sailing warships was sliding into view, following as close on the heels of the galleys as the fluky wind would permit. War engines on their decks were still busy, and Blade saw more of the white spouts of falling projectiles creeping down the pirates' line. The royal navy of Royth was riding in to the attack.

And if he could persuade his crew to resist the natural temptation to simply out oars and run for it, *Charger* could do her share and more. If the galleys on the beach and anchored at the south end of the line had a chance to pull themselves into battle formation, short-handed as they were they might put up a murderous fight. The fleet of Royth might be crippled beyond repair even if victorious. But if *Charger* lived up to her name, hurling herself into the middle of the assembling galleys, she might sow mighty confusion among them. And the royal warfleet might well sweep the whole length of the pirate fleet before effective resistance developed. Blade decided it was worth trying, slim as it left their own chances of survival. He scrambled down to the deck, and called Brora to him.

"Brora, we're going to attack the southern end of the pirate fleet."

Brora turned pale and swallowed, then nodded. He didn't need to spend much more time than Blade thinking out what *Charger* might do—and at what cost. He turned away, bawling orders to the oarmaster and the rowers. The beat of the oars quickened, and Blade felt the timbers under his feet begin to throb with that beat.

So far, no one had connected the sudden attack from Royth with Blade, and *Charger* was moving away unmolested. Behind her the flagship was now ablaze for nearly half her length, and Blade could see the splashes made by sailors hurling themselves from her high decks into the sea. On shore, people were swarming down the beaches and scrambling aboard ships, and a number of the anchored galleys of the inner line were already underway. There was no sign of *Sea Witch* or of Cayla's allies. When Cayla appeared, with or without allies, Blade knew he would have a fight on his hands.

A large galley with black and orange checked sails was turning almost broadside to them as her oarsmen settled to their beat. Blade ran aft and stationed himself alongside the tillermen, while Brora ran forward to speak to the oarmaster and then manned the catapult on the bow. *Charger's* head came around slightly to starboard, aiming for a point nicely calculated to intercept the other galley. The oarsmen bent to their work, the oars thumping in their sockets and the foam curling higher and higher alongside as they worked up to their racing stroke.

The men of the galley ahead had only a brief minute to realize that the other galley racing down on them meant to attack. Blade saw men running on her deck, heard *Charger's* catapult twang and spray a shower of lead slugs into the men on the enemy's deck. Some of them died, others threw themselves flat. Those who had thrown themselves flat were just beginning to rise when *Charger's* ram crashed through her opponent's oars and into her side amidships. Oars cracked, timbers splintered, the enemy's mainmast snapped and went over the side, dragging half the tiller crew with it, men mangled by the ram or by the flailing oars howled and screamed below decks. Brora snapped out orders, and *Charger's* oars went into reverse, pulling her free of the other galley. She was heeling over and sagging low in the water even before *Charger* had come about on a new course in search of a new victim.

This new victim was a smaller galley, as nimble as *Charger* and expecting the attack. Her oarsmen worked furiously, swinging her bows-on to the approaching *Charger*. Blade grinned. He had suggested one or two unorthodox tactics to Brora, who had trained his crew appropriately. Now Brora gave the necessary orders. *Charger's* bow swung until she was aiming her ram down the side of the approaching enemy, then he bellowed, "In all oars, starboard!" The entire starboard crew jerked their oars in through the ports and everybody aboard *Charger* braced themselves as she ploughed along her opponent's side, snapping and splintering the whole bank of oars on that side. The archers on *Charger's* deck had time to add to the enemy's discomfiture with three volleys, then the two ships were pulling apart, *Charger* building up speed again, the other limping away crab-wise.

The catapult fired again, this time hurling a huge wad of oil-soaked rope across the deck of a small merchant-man passing under their lee only fifty yards away. A pinnace with a dozen men in it scuttled across *Charger's* bow, miscalculated its distance, and was trampled underfoot by the rushing galley. Blade saw the men spilled into the water and thrashing wildly to avoid *Charger's* oars, but there was no time to pick up survivors. Arrows, catapult bolts, and stones were beginning to splash down about *Charger* or crash and chunk into her decks as the crews of the ships around her realized that she was an enemy.

A galley came backing off the beach now, moving slowly, with only about half her oars in action. She was keeping such a poor lookout that *Charger* easily darted in and rammed her in the stern, smashing her rudder, then threw a firepot onto her deck as she tried to turn under oars alone. Three down! Blade began to wonder whether the arms of the rowers—or *Charger's* seams—could take the strain of much more high-speed maneuvering and violent ramming.

Then Brora squalled incoherently, with the note of panic in his voice sounding so loud that Blade spun about as though an assassin were striking at his back, whipping his sword free in the same instant. Racing toward them out of the smoke pall laid across the water by the burning flagship was *Sea Witch*. Cayla was clearly visible, perched on the bow just above a ram that was half-submerged in green water by the speed of *Witch's* passage. She had her arms stretched out toward the sea, and as Blade watched, his jaw set, she raised her arms.

Five monstrous fanged heads rose out of the sea, turning inquiringly on the ends of twenty-foot lengths of scaled green neck. Blade saw those heads turn toward *Charger*, felt the glare of five pairs of angry red eyes sear him. Then he instinctively stepped back from the railing as the heads and necks fell back into the water. Five mounds of water rose up where they had been, five mounds arrowing straight for *Charger*. Here were Cayla *and* her allies—here were the Serpent Priestess and the Serpent Guardians—she had summoned them out of the depths of the sea, out of the depths of nightmare. And here was a last deadly battle for life itself.

CHAPTER 21

Whatever arcane skills had conjured these beasts out of their lairs, they were still flesh and blood. Blade was the first to realize this and feel his own cold fear fade, but Brora was the first to act. He leaped back onto the foc'sle where the catapult stood loaded for another shot, swung it around on its pivot, and jerked the firing lanyard. The bolt whistled across the narrowing gap of water and struck one of the creatures a glancing blow on the neck, ripping away scales and part of the long crest of bony spines that ran down its back. It hissed with a fury like a boiler releasing steam, opened its mouth in a wider gape, and came on. But now there was blood flowing down its neck, a green, thick, gluey ichon, whose foul reek came even across the water.

Seeing one of the creatures wounded put new heart in *Charger's* crew. Arrows whistled from bows, bounced off scales, fell into the churning water. Other sailors snatched up javelins and shields and braced themselves to throw.

"Aim for the eyes!" Blade roared. "Ramming speed! Tiller hard a-port!" *Charger* heeled over sharply, throwing some of the men off their feet. Blade was aiming away to the right of the approaching monsters, toward *Sea Witch* and Cayla herself. Slay their mistress and guide, and the serpents would be reduced to mindless hulks of muscle and ferocity, a menace to all and therefore the foe of all. They would not stand or survive in the face of a hundred ships, whatever they might do to *Charger*.

He stared at *Sea Witch,* trying to make out Cayla in the smoke that hung thicker and thicker over the water. She no longer rode her ship's prow like a figurehead; was that she, the slim figure amidships? Yes! Blade ran forward to the catapult and slapped Brora on the arm, pointing toward Cayla. The sailor nodded. "Aye, 'tis finally time to reckon things up with that she-demon!" The catapult went *spung* and its bolt splintered a section of railing beside the figure on *Witch's* deck. But the figure only waved a mocking arm, and then the five monsters were on *Charger* and it was time to fight them off before turning against their mistress.

Charger heaved as though caught in a tidal wave as three of the creatures rose under her, tilting so far over that one whole bank of oars thrashed the air futilely. The fighting men on deck either held onto things or were tossed wildly down the length of her deck. Two of them clawed at splintered lengths of railing, missed, went over the side with a splash. A fanged head turned their way, lifted, dipped, plunged into the sea in a spray of foam and blood, its hisses drowning their screams. Then *Charger* lurched back the other way, and those who had kept their feet during the first heave went sailing into the bilges in a clatter of weapons and gear.

All except Blade and Brora. They clung like monkeys in a tree to the catapult, and as one of the creatures threw a yard-thick coil into the air, skewered it with a point-blank bolt. The air split apart with a hiss of agony, foam and blood showered them, and the writhing creature hurled itself at them, jaws opened to seize, the head smashing like a battering ram into the catapult. It flew to pieces, and in the seconds when the half-stunned creature's head lay motionless in the wreckage, Blade lunged for-

171

ward and drove his sword deep through one glaring red eye into the brain. The beast convulsed in one gigantic jerk that whipped the six-foot head forward almost to Blade's feet, fanged jaws snapping in a final spasm, then lurched over the side and vanished.

Blade and Brora bent to pick up axes—more suitable for this butcher's work because more robust—then spun around as screams sounded from aft. The oarsmen had snatched up their weapons and armor and were pouring up onto the deck. The fanged jaws closed on one sailor, crumpling his armor and crunching his bones in a single motion; twenty feet of its body swept like a giant flail across the deck, knocking another half-dozen off their feet. One brave soul rolled clear, snatched up a javelin, ran forward, drove it into the back of the serpent's skull. The monster dropped its first victim in bloody rags on the deck, turned to confront this new opponent. As it did so Blade and Brora ran in, one on each side, waving their axes. The two broad iron heads came down, splintering the skull and chopping through the spine and a foot into the massive body. The creature died without a further motion, the sheer weight of its body dragging it over the side.

With two of her allies slain and a third wounded, Blade wondered for a moment if Cayla might not call them off for a space. But it seemed that the woman on *Sea Witch's* deck was now driven by a lust for blood and vengeance only a little less mindless than the hunger and fury which drove her serpents. At least she could guide them into a more cunning attack than the headlong charge they had used until now.

This time, the three survivors came on together. It seemed that the sea itself had risen against *Charger* as the creatures hurled themselves out of the water to smash down on her decks like falling trees, pulping the men caught underneath, sweeping others overboard, flailing and thrashing about. Their weight dragged *Charger* down until her lee rail was only a few feet above the water, their hissing deafened, their musky odor clawed at Blade's nose and throat, their thrashing made the deck seams gape and the hull timbers groan.

172

Blade saw that he and Brora were alone on *Charger's* deck now and that the ship herself was coming apart under the punishment the three monsters were inflicting. A few more minutes of this, and he and Brora would be swimming for their lives in the water, where any of the serpents could pluck them up as easily as a fish. He had forgotten about the larger battle, forgotten even to care whether Royth was winning or losing, in the struggle against the serpents.

He and Brora backed as far forward as they could go and looked at each other. Even now, Brora hefted his axe and grinned savagely. Under their feet the deck gave another lurch, and Blade felt the bow rise higher out of the water as the creatures writhed their way aft and pressed the stern down into the water. The water would be flooding through the stern windows now, dragging *Charger* deeper and deeper.

There were a few remaining catapult bolts lying on the tilting deck along with the rest of the debris. Six feet long and steel-tipped, they were clumsy but serviceable spears. Blade bent to pick one up, saw Brora do the same. He hefted his, testing it for balance. The sun flashed on its head, flashed into the eyes of one of the beasts until now too concerned with obeying its orders to smash the ship down into the sea. It lifted its head, opened its mouth, swelled out its sides and throat with a deadly hissing. Then it lunged.

Blade and Brora leaped aside. Blade saw his companion backed up against the opposite railing, saw his mouth open in a scream as the creature's head swung toward him. Then Blade shut everything else out of his mind, concentrating only on placing his thrust and his axe blow as he hurled himself forward for the kill.

He moved so fast that his bolt skittered across the scales of the head, flew out of his hand and over the side. He sprawled headlong across the creature's back as his axe came down, chopping through scales and flesh and into the spine. The hiss of the creature in its death agony almost deafened him, and the putrid green mud that gushed forth from the wound seared his skin like scalding

173

water and choked him like the odor of a cesspool. Half-blinded, he clawed at the creature's scales for a handhold as it reared up, until the dangling head was thirty feet above the deck. Then the serpent twisted in its final convulsion, flinging Blade high into the air like a stone from a sling.

Clinging by instinct to his axe, he saw the water coming up, felt it slam him across face and body, and kicked out furiously the moment he hit. But he went far under, far enough to see the weeds wriggling on the sandy bottom, far enough so that when he turned on his back and looked up the surface was a silver roof over a gray-green cave. Then he was struggling upward toward the surface, kicking off his boots as he went, dropping his belt and trousers, coming to the surface clad only in his shirt. He stripped that off with two quick motions of his free hand and looked about him.

He had expected that the two remaining serpents would be on him the moment he hit the water, but he suddenly realized that Cayla might not have seen him hurtle through the air and plunge under the water. If that were the case, she would not know to call her allies off from their job of sinking *Charger* to comb the waters about her for Blade. As long as he was invisible to Cayla he might have a chance of safety. He turned his head and began scanning around him for *Witch*. The murk of gray-brown smoke, spreading now from other burning ships besides the flagship, ebbed and flowed across the surface of the water. It made his eyes sting all over again and reduced the ships about him to lurking wraith-shapes.

He saw *Charger*, her ram now jutting green and slimy from the water as the writhings of the great serpents dragged her farther and farther down, churning the water white about her now-submerged stern. Bodies and wreckage were floating away from her as she dipped lower. He saw no sign of Brora. But he knew that in the murk the half-sighted monsters would have little hope of detecting anything more than fifty feet from their scaled noses without their mistress' aid. If Brora had clawed his way clear

174

of the sinking ship, he might be hundreds of yards away by now and safe.

He turned back toward the flagship, in the direction where he had last seen *Witch,* and saw only the smoke and a skiff making her cautious way through the murk under oars. Then, turning farther, he saw two ships grappled together—a galley of Royth and a pirate galley beyond her—their decks a mass of struggling figures. He blinked water out of his eyes and looked again. Was one of the figures standing apart from the mass slim, with a head of hair so blonde and fair it gleamed even in the murk? Yes! His powerful legs churned the water behind him as he hurled himself through the water like a human torpedo toward the two ships. As he closed the distance, his few doubts vanished—here was Cayla, here was the final reckoning with the she-demon! Would tough and faithful Brora ever know about it?

The battle on the ships' decks had risen to its climax as Blade pulled himself alongside the Royth galley. Every few seconds a living man or a dead body would topple over the side, to strike out frantically or sink or drift away. Blade seized a rope trailing over the side, braced his feet against the weed-slick planks of the galley's hull, and scrambled up onto the deck.

He took a few seconds to size up the situation. In that few seconds the men ramping and struggling on the deck had time to turn and notice the apparition that had burst onto their deck—a colossal naked man, with skin burnt dark by sun and wind stretched over masses of rippling muscles, swinging an axe in one hand as though it were as light as a quill pen. Then he bellowed "Cayla!" in a terrible roaring voice and charged forward. Pirates and navymen sprang aside from his path.

Blade's few seconds of observation had told his trained eye that here at least the pirates had the edge of it, having hurled the navy boarding parties back onto their own decks and then gone over to the attack. He crossed the galley's quarterdeck in a half dozen long strides, the axe whirling in his right hand, and sprang down onto the main deck in a single bound. Once again he was a killing machine, and now the small part of him still fully rational knew that Cayla was almost within his grasp, and both reason and the urge to kill drove him onward together at a frightening pace.

A pirate whirled, aiming a sword thrust at Blade's stomach. Blade danced to one side, brought the axe up, saw the head sink into the man's stomach, and felt the handle smash into his arm. The man's sword flew into the air. Blade snatched it from the deck and parried a pike thrust with it almost in the same motion. Another pirate ran at Blade, also wielding a pike. Blade feinted left with the sword, brought the axe up as the pirate responded, then leaped aside and brought it down on the man's skull. The pirate was dead before he hit the deck and Blade sprang over the falling body to engage two more.

One of these had a shield and Blade launched a kick at the man's knee to force the shield down, then thrust over the top into his face with the sword. Simultaneously he whipped the axe up in time to take the other pirate's frantic downstroke on the axe-head. Sparks flew, metal clanged, the shock half-numbed Blade's arm. But the other pirate's sword flew from his hand and before he could leap back Blade swung his left arm with the bloody sword across and thrust the man through the belly.

Blade had now cleared a space around him, and the pirates were beginning to lose heart, while fore and aft the navymen were rallying. A pirate rushed at Blade with a mace swinging in both hands and died clutching at an arrow rammed through his throat by a navy archer on the foc'sle. Two more pirates fell off the foc'sle, landing hard enough to be stunned for a moment. Blade was on them in seconds, axe swinging. A reluctance to slaughter half-stunned men like pigs made him shift his grip on the haft just enough so that the flat of the blade, not the edge, struck them down to the deck again.

Then from both forward and aft, the navymen charged out in a full-scale counterattack, the bowmen dropping their bows and pulling out daggers and swords and engaging in a fight so utterly entangled that even Blade was hard put to tell friend from foe. There was a wild moment

176

of balance, when the kettle-mending sound of clashing steel rose to a deafening din. Thrusts and slashes came at Blade so fast that in that moment all even he could do was parry and dodge and occasionally wince as steel slashed his bare skin. He was bleeding from half a dozen minor wounds when a trumpet blared close in his ear. The pirates gave way, those who still could move fast enough. Blade saw them dashing for the railing, leaping up on it, and hurling themselves across to the comparative safety of *Witch's* deck.

And beyond them, for the first time since he boarded the galley, Blade saw Cayla standing out straight and proud amid the swirl of battle and the retreat of her crew. With no thought of odds or anything else except coming to grips with her, he sprang onto the railing and leaped across onto *Witch's* deck.

Once again, men drew back at Blade's appearance. Naked, blood-smeared, eyes blazing with fury, he cleared a space around him by his mere presence, without a single stroke of sword or axe. But Cayla saw her crew giving way before Blade and screamed out in a voice raw and shrill with fury:

"There is only one, and he is only a man! Are *you* men?" As if wakened from a trance, the pirates sprang to life and hurled themselves against Blade.

He almost went down under the assault; there were at least fifteen coming against him, and he had already been fighting men and monsters for hours, apart from his wounds. He had to give way in his turn, retreating to the railing and making his stand there, sword and axe whirling like some deadly machine. The barrier they made between him and his opponents was impenetrable. Even worse for the pirates, at any slackening of the attack sword or axe would leap out into their ranks, a deadly tongue of steel licking out, smashing, ripping, maiming. There were so many of the pirates that they blundered into each other's way as they sought to get at Blade, and to make a blunder against Blade was a death sentence. There were fifteen pirates to begin with, then twelve, then ten.

Blade found a moment to appreciate the fact that he was nearing the end of his adventure in this Dimension as he had begun it—fighting single-handed against a mass of Neraler pirates. But he was filled with yet more fury that these poor fools he kept smashing down to the deck were keeping him from getting at Cayla. There were moments when a pause in the swirl of bodies before him let him see her, standing with one hand on her hip and the other urging her men on with flourishes of her sword. Then she disappeared for a time, and when he saw her again, she was stalking away down *Witch's* deck, hands busy with the straps and buckles of her armor. At that sight Blade's fury boiled still higher, and he bellowed like a bull and launched himself like a battering-ram against the men in front of him, lunging under sword and pike strokes.

The sheer impact of his giant body hurtling forward at full speed threw half the men opposing him to the deck, some of them stunned. Before the others could rally and block his path again or attack his now undefended rear, navymen from the Royth galley alongside began to swarm over the railings to join the battle. Blade turned for a moment to watch them and nearly died for his curiosity, as Cayla sprang around in a complete half-turn as graceful as a ballet dancer's and lunged at him. Her light sword was razor-sharp. It ripped open his right arm deep enough to make him gasp. The axe fell from his suddenly limp fingers and crashed to the deck. He brought the sword up to parry another lunge, but instead Cayla ran lightly forward until she was at the foc'sle. She leaped up on the railing, kicking off her boots as she did so, and gave a wild cry ending in a sibilant note that made Blade's flesh crawl. Then she shrugged her unbuckled cuirass off, leaving herself bare to the waist. She threw up one slim arm in a mocking gesture to Blade, sending her sword flying through the air. As he ducked aside, she sprang from the railing and vanished over the side.

She was already many yards ahead of Blade by the time he hit the water and rose from his dive to follow her, and she was gaining every second. She might have been easy to overtake for Blade at his full strength, but he was far from fresh, and his disabled arm slowed him down even though he had also dropped his axe. But his remaining arm, his legs, and a single desperate thought drove him ahead at a muscle-wrenching, throat-searing pace. It was the thought that he must catch up with Cayla, must silence or stun her, before her serpent allies could respond to her call to rise out of whatever part of this bloody sea they now swam through and destroy him.

He soon realized she was making straight for shore. She was keeping well ahead of him, but the gap between them was no longer widening, and she had never found a second chance to pause and call the serpents. On and on they churned, through water now spotted thickly with floating bodies, balks of timber, masts complete with sails and rigging, overturned boats, odd bits of wood, and personal gear. Again, Blade felt he was ending this adventure as he had begun it—swimming through a wreckage-strewn sea—and again reminded himself that the true end to it all swam twenty yards ahead of him, white limbs thrashing along as tirelessly as his own.

Then he saw Cayla lurch to her feet, turn toward the sea, and give her serpent call again, now with a note of desperation that came clear even to Blade's water-deafened ears. And this time it was answered, as two hideously familiar heads writhed their way up out of the sea fifty yards off to the right.

Blade for a moment kept going by sheer reflex, as the prospect of those fanged, slime-dripping jaws closing on his body made him turn chill all over. Then he was churning through the water even faster, angling off to the left but still heading toward shore. He was swimming for life itself now; if he could get ashore safely he might find a weapon or at least a chance to outrun the two monsters, a chance he would never find in the water. He swam until he was certain that *both* arms would snap off like rotten twigs if he lifted them for another stroke, until his chest felt as though one of the giant serpents was already coiled around it, until he could almost feel the joints of his hips

179

and legs squeal protestingly as he forced them to keep moving.

It seemed that the minutes had already stretched into hours and the hours were stretching into days, when he felt solid bottom strike his feet. By reflex alone he changed his legs' motion from swimming to a staggering run. He splashed through the water, and behind him another splashing sounded, growing louder and louder. He was out on the hard-packed sand of the beach now, running like a hare, his eyes darting from right to left, searching less for possible enemies than for loose weapons he might snatch up. He would not worry about human opponents now; what was slithering out of the sea behind him was a far more deadly danger.

A low rise loomed ahead, and behind him he heard the splashing die away in favor of a grating noise of scales on sand as the monsters writhed their way up onto the beach. He topped the rise, tripped, went face down in the sand, rolled down into a hollow, and fetched up hard against an abandoned tent. Cautiously he rose to hands and knees and peered inside the tent—then grinned. The tent was full of barrels and bales, except for the center, where a hastily-pegged-together rack held a long row of spears and pikes, some upright and some lying flat. There was no one to stop him as he darted in and snatched up three twelve-foot spears.

Now it was his turn to attack. Keeping low, he crawled up the tumbled sand and peered through a clump of beach grass. To the north was nothing but a swirling gray-brown wall, fed by fires both afloat and ashore, with the northern breeze drifting the murk thicker and thicker toward where he lay. He could see nothing and hear little to suggest how the battle was going elsewhere. He cared even less, for his own private fight was not yet finished.

Cayla herself now stood ankle deep in the water, entirely nude. The two great serpents were coiled up on the beach in front of her, with perhaps the rear thirty feet of their bodies still submerged and their vast heads swaying gently back and forth some ten feet above the sand. Their mouths open and shut as she spoke to them in the half-bark, half-hiss Blade now knew so well. Behind her, drifting in toward shore, bobbed a great tangle of planks, spars, and canvas. Blade rose to his knees and hefted a spear. It was not his preference to kill an unarmed woman, but far too many attempts to kill *him* lay between them, and from this distance it would in any case be folly to try for a disabling shot. He might well miss entirely and have the serpents on him in seconds. He sprang to his feet and hurled the spear.

It was a good throw but not good enough. The spear grazed Cayla's hip and skittered into the water behind her. Before the ripples of its fall had vanished, she spun about, thrust out a hand toward Blade, and screamed out triumphantly. Blade snatched up the second spear and ran at the nearer serpent before it had time to uncoil most of itself. The head was still hovering uncertainly in the air as the flaring red eyes sought to focus on its prey when Blade ran in under that head, leaped as high as he could, and thrust the spear into the monster's throat.

Again a death-hiss tore at Blade's ears, again the fumes of the thing's blood tore at his lungs and stung his skin. He let go of the spearshaft barely in time to avoid being hurled into the air, as the monster reared up with the spear still embedded in its throat and lunged toward the sea. But he did not avoid its flailing coils entirely, as a yard-thick section of body whipped out and slammed into him hard enough to hurl him to the sand.

He saw the other monster rear up, clawed frantically backward to get at the remaining spear, then heard Cayla's cry of triumph change to a gasp and a bubbling scream. He lurched to his feet with the last spear in his hand and saw Cayla staggering, the point of a pike jutting from her body just below the left breast. A blood-smeared, smoke-blackened figure stood just behind her, and as Blade watched the figure jerked the pike free and thrust it into Cayla again. This time she went face down into the water, which instantly turned red about her thrashing limbs. As the figure stood over her and raised the pike for a third thrust, Blade recognized the face, darkened as it was by blood, smoke, and rage.

181

"Brora! Enough!"

"Captain Blahyd!" Brora turned, showed white teeth in a smile, and took a single step toward Blade. Then the last serpent, no longer under the control of its dying mistress, no longer responding to anything except hunger and rage, turned and noticed the two figures almost beneath its head. The head dipped, lunged downward, and Brora's final scream mingled with Cayla's as both vanished in a flurry of water. The creature's jaws snapped shut and blood began to spread in the water; then Blade sprinted across the sand and through the water to drive his last spear into the snake's eyesocket.

It reared up in a final agony, letting its prey drop as the blood-dripping jaws sagged open. Blade had one good look at what Cayla and Brora had become, then turned and ran as though the flames of hell were licking at his heels, back onto the dry beach, back up the slope and down the other side into the tent. There, and there only, he finally collapsed, too spent even to be sick, too deaf to the world to hear the final thrashings of the last of Cayla's monsters.

What broke into his semi-oblivion was an unexpected but not unfamiliar sound—the sound of somebody calling cadence, accompanied by the rhythmic thump of a large body of men coming down the beach in step. Such a style of marching did not suggest to Blade a mob of fleeing pirates or camp-followers. It was with as much jauntiness as his sagging limbs could muster up that he went out to greet the approaching men.

It was no surprise to see two companies of the Royal Guard of Royth coming down the beach at full march step, weapons drawn and scouts thrown out in front. But what was a surprise was to see Tralthos tramping along at their head. And Tralthos was equally surprised when he recognized the preposterous figure that tottered into view, naked as the day of its birth, as the Constable Blahyd.

Blade had regained enough energy and had enough sense of the dignity of the occasion to keep from falling on his face a second time as he and Tralthos embraced each other and pounded each other on the back. But after that he had to sit down, and Tralthos followed him. They squatted on the sand while Tralthos told Blade of the great victory of Royth.

"We got out of the Keltz as easy as eating a gooseberry tart and hugged the coast all the way south, moving by night. Last night we sent some tough lads ashore from the fleet to take out the sentries on that little peninsula up north—" Blade nodded as Tralthos pointed "—and mounted some of our engines up there. This morning, we got the galleys around the point and in through a deep passage the local pilots knew about but the pirates didn't. Then we just rolled up their line from the north while the merchantmen went farther out and kept their big ships from getting away. I think we must have sunk or burned or captured more than three hundred ships. The admiral decided a couple of hours ago we might as well land some troops to clean up the camp, so he ran the transports inshore and unloaded the two battalions of the Guard he had along."

Blade nodded. As with any brief account of a great battle, he knew that Tralthos was leaving two-thirds of it out. But Blade was not sure that his fogged mind and aching head could take in any more. But also:

"What about the army?"

Tralthos' grin broadened still further. "Horsemen with messages rode over the bluff not half an hour ago. Said we'd put four brigades between the pirates and the beach and the other five on their front and right. If they're smart, they'll surrender now. If not, it'll take a while to kill them all, but there won't be anything left but bandits in another two weeks."

Blade nodded again. He had no more questions at this point and no energy to ask them even if he had. But Tralthos was going on.

"Pelthros is on his way back to High Royth posthaste. Can't wait to get back to his crafts, I wager, now that he doesn't need to be a big fighting man any more. He'd still rather leave that to people like you and me. But you'll be getting more rewards for this, believe me! He'll be lucky if

the people let him get away with making you a count!
And when you marry Alixa—"

But Blade suddenly could no longer hear the cheerful
soldier. The ache in his head suddenly flared up to the
point of driving in on his fatigue-dulled consciousness,
flared to an agonizing wrenching as the computer reached
out across the dimensions to snatch him home. He could
no longer even sit; he was falling face down on the sand.

Then the sand that he was digging up with his clawing
fingers and toes turned completely over, and he was clinging to the roof of a vast chamber, filled with a murky
green vapor that curled about him. Half-hidden in the vapor, Tralthos and his soldiers hung head-down from the
same ceiling, like bats from the ceiling of a cave. And
then they were bats, squeaking and beating their wings
and darting off to become lost in the darkness.

A light appeared below, soft and pearly, spreading out,
taking shape, taking the shape of Alixa, her proud body
bare, rising toward Blade. And Blade let himself fall away
from the sandy ceiling, down, down toward Alixa, down
into her, down through, down into the murk that suddenly
lost all its tint of green and turned cold and black.

CHAPTER 22

"And now," said J as he and Lord Leighton settled
themselves in armchairs, "I think it's high time we
thrashed out some questions this last mission has raised."

"Certainly, certainly," replied the scientist, opening a
cabinet beside his chair and pulling out a bottle and glass-
es. "Would you care for some brandy?"

J shook his head. "Not now, thank you." They were in
a small but lavishly furnished waiting room, part of the
hospital complex that lay a further hundred feet down below the computer room under the Tower. Three rooms
away, Richard Blade, bathed, bandaged, and electronically monitored down to the slightest wiggle of his little

finger, was sleeping peacefully. It was a hypnotically induced sleep, into which he had been sent after finishing
his narrative of his latest adventure in Dimension X. It
was this adventure and some particularly disturbing things
about it that J wanted to thrash out with Lord Leighton.

Lord Leighton poured himself a small glass of brandy
and sniffed at it, then set it on the cabinet and made a
steeple of his thin fingers. "I hope you realize that the
chronic distortion involved in this mission is a very disturbing phenomenon. Previously we have had a one-to-one
congruence between X Dimension and Home Dimension
time. That is, if Blade felt nine months had passed in Dimension X, nine months had also passed here. But now
Blade comes back after what was the better part of a year
to him, and only *four months* have passed here. The
chronic distortion has reached two for one or more for the
first time we encounter it."

J nodded. That was indeed one of the matters he wanted to discuss with Lord L but not the principal one.
"Frankly, I think what we need to consider is whether we
had any reason to keep him there so long at all. If he had
returned after only—"

"Quite true, quite true," said Lord Leighton, in a tone
of voice that J recognized as actually admitting nothing of
the kind. "But we have to consider this in the perspective
of repeated missions. Suppose the next time we get a distortion but in the reverse direction? Let us say Blade stays
in Dimension X a time that is for him only a few days,
but several months pass here. It lends an extremely disturbing element of unpredictability to the whole Project."

"As if we didn't have enough already," said J rather
sourly. He was not particularly interested in running to
earth this particular hare that Leighton had started. But
he held his peace for nearly ten minutes while the scientist
wandered off into totally unintelligible realms of technical
and scientific abstraction. Even Lord Leighton, and even
when discussing a scientific topic dear to his heart, could
run out of things to say, however. When this finally happened, J was ready.

"It's all very well to worry about things we *can't* con-

185

trol—oh, very well, that we can't control *now*—but the more immediate problem is something else. Richard was gone nearly nine months, came as close to being killed as he ever has—and for what? The people in that Dimension were, frankly, a collection of the most unprepossessing specimens I've ever heard of. Life there seems to have been 'dull, nasty, brutish and short,' but Richard spent nine whole months there, helping them to solve a perfectly ordinary problem with pirates that they probably could have handled just as well themselves."

Leighton sipped his brandy and nodded.

"My God, Leighton, when I think of how close we came to losing him in some squalid little affair with a mess of pirates. . . . Pirates!" He uttered the word as though it were the blackest obscenity he could think of.

J was still shaking his head in disgust when a nurse entered, trim and crisp in her hospital uniform. "Excuse me, gentlemen. Mr. Blade is awake and asking for both of you."

Leighton laboriously pulled himself out of the chair and stood up. "Well, then, since Richard is awake, why don't you ask him yourself?"

"Eh?"

"Did *he* think it was worthwhile, getting involved in that 'squalid little affair'?"

They followed the nurse out of the waiting room and down the hall to Blade's room. He was sitting up in bed, looking tired but cheerful, and greeted them warmly as they entered. After the initial handshakings, Leighton looked at J with a well-why-don't-you-ask-him expression written all over his face. J cleared his throat, looked first at the ceiling, then at the floor, then finally at Blade, and said:

"Richard, there's something I've been meaning to ask you about this last affair. Did you think it was worth it, in terms of what Project Dimension X set out to do?"

"Meaning exploring the various phases of Dimension X to bring back things of value for England's use?"

"That's one way of putting it, yes."

Blade appeared to be having an unusual amount of

trouble phrasing his answer. He grimaced, frowned, pulled at his lower lip for a time, then said, "Yes, sir, I think it was. In an odd sort of way, I'll admit. There's nothing that I can see wrong with exploring these X Dimensions for England and bringing back materials and techniques for our use here. But it seems to me that we ought to be able to offer them something in return. Since we haven't yet worked out a way to take anything material through the computer transfer, the next best thing seems to me the sort of thing I just did—helping them cope with their problems. Sometimes I have a perspective on the problem that they don't, or skills, or something like that. And this wasn't the first time I've spent extra time helping the local people. Remember Tharn? Or the Gnomen?"

J did. Lord Leighton smiled. "I see your point, Richard. Well, as long as you are willing to keep at it, you'll have plenty of opportunities to arrange your little aid-for-trade exchanges. And now, I think you look like you need some more sleep." He ushered J out into the corridor and closed the door behind them, then turned to the other and grinned impishly.

"I rather suspected Blade was going to say what he did, so I let him say it. I agree with him absolutely, but of course I knew you'd take it much better from him than from me."

"Well, I'll be damned!" said J, in frank amazement. "You *are* getting to be a romantic altruist in your old age!"

This time Leighton's grin was more sheepish than impish. "Better late than never, eh?"

"No doubt. But if you're going to indulge this notion of running the Project as a sort of interdimensional welfare agency, I think it would be wise to step up the search for more candidates besides Richard. Everything I've already said on that point still stands."

In the monitored hospital bed, Richard Blade was not worrying about the Project or the need for other people to take his place in it. He was thinking of Royth and above all of Alixa. Beautiful, passionate, level-headed. Of all the memories he would have of Royth, she was the one he

187

would not lose. Alixa, yes, and Brora, tough, loyal, putting an end to Cayla at the cost of his own life and willingly so. And Tuabir. He was glad he and Lord L seemed to see eye-to-eye on the point he had raised. There were people in each of the multitude of worlds in Dimension X who deserved help, who would get it from him whenever he could, however he could. This brought his mind back to his first sight of Alixa, then their first bout of love, and presently he fell asleep.